"What could a woman and a man, alone, have to do with train robberies?" the redhead asked.

"I'm not so sure you *are* alone." Spur might not be able to read them completely, but he knew they were lying. "Start talking, fast, or I'll blow your brains out!"

The two stared at him in surprise, then terror.

"No!" the woman said. "I never did anything! I wasn't even with them!"

"Shut your mouth, Phoebe!" the boy said.

"What are you talking about? You never did what? Who's 'them'?"

"I . . . I only cooked for them. That's all!"

"Quiet!" the blond boy snarled at her.

"That's enough, kid!" Spur slashed the .45 across the boy's forehead, jolting him backward. "Tell me, Phoebe. What meals? For whom? The two of you?"

"Jesus Christ, Phoebe, shut your dumb mouth!" The boy shook with anger.

"There are more of us," the redhead blurted.

"Damn you" growled the kid, making a lunge for her.

"Don't move." Spur swung the Colt .45 to cover him.

"And don't *you* move, stranger, or you'll get six rounds in your back!" a loud female voice boomed from behind Spur.

Also in the *Spur* Series:

SPUR #12

GOLD TRAIN TRAMP

DIRK FLETCHER

LEISURE BOOKS NEW YORK CITY

A LEISURE BOOK®

April 2004

Published by

Dorchester Publishing Co., Inc.
200 Madison Avenue
New York, NY 10016

ISBN 0-8439-2283-4

The name "Leisure Books" and the stylized "L" with design are
trademarks of Dorchester Publishing Co., Inc.

Printed in the United States of America.

Visit us on the web at www.dorchesterpub.com.

GOLD TRAIN TRAMP

CHAPTER ONE

Southern Wyoming Territory, April 1870

Ray Lloyd slid on his belly up to the cliff's edge and lifted his head to peer over it. Stretching away from him, the black ribbon of the railroad tracks slanted downward and disappeared into the early morning mist and heavy fog. He soon heard the first soft patterings of the distant train.

Lloyd had seen enough. He pushed his six-foot frame back from the edge and scrambled down the cliff, rejoining his two partners. They cleared twenty yards of open ground, each man clutching one empty saddle bag.

They crouched behind a huge boulder ten feet from the tracks. The sound of the approaching train grew in intensity. Lloyd grinned and looked at his two men. Just a few more seconds.

The train swiftly appeared from the fog, its oil fueled head lamp shining wanly in the brightening sunshine. Greasy black coal smoke shot up from the stacks at the ends of the twin engines. As they bit away at the steep mountain grade the train slowed from its full throttle speed of forty miles per hour to less than ten.

Lloyd listened to the engine's slowly lengthening rhythm. It was almost time. He adjusted the kerchief tied around his face and tightened the knot—no need taking chances.

He glanced at Robinson and Willis. The blond kid's eyes shone; his heart beat with excitement. He was confident and bold. Robinson, the older man, was grim, determined. Good, Lloyd thought. It should be a good job. He checked his Colt. It was fully loaded and ready to help out a needy friend.

The train's first engine had just cleared the boulder. Lloyd looked up; moments later the second engine passed behind him, shaking the earth and pounding the air with grinding drive wheels, clanging rods and hissing steam.

The three men sprang from behind the boulder and ran beside the train, which still slowly climbed the hill. They jumped onto the vestibule to the rear of the last passenger car. Lloyd pulled open the door and stormed in while the others followed him.

Twelve passengers looked up with mild interest—until Lloyd leveled a Colt at the ground and cleared his throat.

"All right, folks. No one's going to get hurt. Just do what we say. Otherwise, we'll blow you all to hell."

A man near the rear of the car raised a hand toward the emergency cord. Robinson and Lloyd trained their weapons on him; the man pulled his arm down fast.

"First rule!" Lloyd said. "If anyone reaches up to pull that cord, I'll kill him. Plain and simple." He surveyed the dozen passengers, three-quarters of whom were men, the rest women, some with babies, and children.

"No!" a young woman screamed. She leapt to her feet. "No!"

Two babies cried in their frightened mother's arms. A burly man reached for his right side nervously, his bald pate shiny with sweat.

Lloyd saw the movement and blasted a round into the man's arm.

"Christ!" the passenger yelled.

"Nobody move!" Lloyd shouted.

"I was just reaching for my cigars," he bellowed in agony. "Shit!" Blood erupted onto his coat sleeve.

"Is this what you mean by not harming anyone?" A stylishly dressed older woman asked, her face white with horror.

"Shut up!" Lloyd pulled off his hat and handed it to a young man sitting in the seat closest to him. "Put your wallets, purses, jewelry, watches and money into that hat, then pass it around. Now. Hurry!"

The nervous youth dumped in his few coins and passed it behind him. Robinson walked down the aisle as the hat moved among the passengers. It filled quickly and Robinson dumped it into a saddle bag, then handed it to the next passenger. The elderly woman took the hat in her unsteady hands and poured the contents of her small beaded purse into it, then passed it behind her.

"That pin," Robinson said, his revolver pointing to the gold brooch at the front of the woman's dress. It sparkled with jewels. "Throw it in."

The woman frowned, sending up riots of wrinkles around her mouth, then removed it and placed it in the hat with trembling fingers.

Robinson smiled and motioned for her to pass that hat.

Lloyd stood cool and easy, watching the Stetson fill again. The people were tense, nervous, but not liable to cause problems. Maybe they wouldn't have any bad trouble this time. The passengers—even the men—acted like sheep. Maybe they were from back east, or just wanted to save their hides. It was almost too easy, Lloyd thought.

When the hat had finished circulating among the passengers Robinson poured the loot into the leather bag and handed it to Lloyd. The two men backed toward the rear door, leaving Willis to stand near the forward entrance, covering the passengers and preventing anyone from entering from the connecting car. Robinson covered the rear.

Lloyd opened the door, stepped outside, and carefully pulled a stick of dynamite from his coat pocket. He checked the cap and fuse, lodged it against the express car's door handle, cupped his hand and lit a match, then touched it to the fuse end. He stepped back into the passenger car and slammed the door shut behind him. Robinson, his full attention turned to the passengers who sat quite still, jumped as the door burst open. A second later the car shook as the dynamite exploded.

"They've blown the safe!" a young boy said excitedly and looked behind him.

"Don't turn around!" Robinson ordered.

The kid swung back forward.

Robinson and Lloyd left Willis in charge of the

passenger car and ran to the express car. The door had shattered and swung open. As Lloyd walked in his blasted the car's interior with four rounds from his Colt. The acrid dynamite smoke cleared, revealing the express man huddled in a corner, apparently unharmed. He glanced nervously at his rifle, which had been thrown across the car.

"For God's sake, don't kill me!" the man said as Robinson bore down on him.

Lloyd went to the twin safes sitting side by side near the small stove provided there for the express man's comfort. "What're the combinations?" Lloyd asked.

"I don't know."

"Mother fuckin' liar!"

"Shut up, Robinson!" Lloyd said. "Tell us or I'll blow your balls off!" He produced another stick of dynamite, unwrapping it carefully from the folds of protective cloth he'd used to cushion the unstable substance.

Sweat poked out from the man's face. His breathing was ragged, harsh—the breath of a man who knows he's about to die.

"Shit!" Robinson said.

The express man jumped to his feet and dove for the rifle. Just before his fingers closed around it Lloyd's Winchester punched a round hole through the express man's forehead. He slammed against the side of the car and gazed up lifelessly at Robinson.

"Come on!" the man said.

Lloyd wedged the stick of dynamite between the heart-shaped lock and the side of the safe. He repeated the process on the other, carefully handling the dynamite, then lit both thirty-second fuses. They ran from the car to the landing and held their hands over their ears. Fifteen seconds later—much too soon—the air shattered with sound. They pushed back in through the smoke.

One safe's door had swung open, and the other was loose. They pried it away. Coughing, Robinson removed the eight bags of $20 gold double eagles and handed them to Lloyd, who stuffed three into each of the bags. Two others had split open, and gold discs lay scattered over the floor.

"Should we—" Robinson began.

"No time." They strapped the bags shut, slung them over their shoulders, and ran from the express car. Lloyd knocked on the window of the door to the passenger car to alert Willis, then jumped from the train.

Shots fired from the firearm atop the coal car flew wide as Lloyd and Robinson darted across the ground, Willis closing in behind. The train continued to rumble up the mountain, while the fireman peppered the ground with inaccurate shooting. Any minute Lloyd knew he might hear the air brakes scream into action, but by that time they'd be gone.

"Come on!" Lloyd shouted.

Willis took a bag from an overloaded Robinson as they stumbled down the steep incline away from the tracks and ran to the hidden valley.

Fear stabbed through Lloyd for a flashing second, a fear that boiled like acid in his gut. Would the horses be there? Or would they be stranded in the middle of nowhere, miles from their hideout, weighed down with gold while Union Pacific employees scoured the hills for them?

Lloyd thought of his alternate plan, the one he'd

worked out years ago. If such a thing happened he'd calmly kill his partners—at present, Steve Robinson and Chuck Willis—bury their bodies, hide the gold and hole up somewhere until it was safe to retrieve the money. But that was only if the unthinkable happened.

They entered the stand of pines and firs that filled the valley—and Lloyd saw the four horses. He sighed.

"Everything go okay?" their mounted fourth member asked in a Texan accent.

"Sure," he said. They transferred the gold to the horses and rode from the valley, back into the foothills of the Rocky Mountains to lose themselves in a land of endless valleys and mountains, shadows and bright patches of sunlight, virgin forests and rushing streams.

"How much did you get?"

Lloyd turned and looked at Suzanna—even this close it was hard to see she was a woman, with her hair pulled under the hat and her fine body hidden beneath the drab pants and shirt. But the voice gave her away every time.

"All the payroll except two bags and some jewelry and money."

"How much altogether?" Suzanna demanded, her eyes flashing.

"Later." He pulled out in front of her.

They rode hard down the slopes, leaving the tracks far behind them.

"Damn you!" Suzanna Buckland said, jumping from her horse and pulling off the low-brimmed Stetson, sending her straight, shoulder length red hair tumbling down around her face. In the full sunlight

13

she was more beautiful, her clear green eyes contrasting sharply with her tresses. Under the clothes her body hinted of delectable curves. Though she was tall, almost 5'8", she wasn't hard or unfeminine because of it; her height only added to her beauty.

"What now?" Lloyd asked sarcastically as they dismounted in a thicket near their hideout, a forgotten, worked-out mine near a stream.

"What do you think?" She looked at the man. Ray Lloyd was forty, in good physical shape, with a craggy face whose scars commemorated meetings with unfriendly fists and blades. Black hair showed under his hat, and as he pulled the kerchief from his lower face and wiped his mouth, Suzanna again marvelled at the strength of his chin and jaw, and the thick moustache that gleamed like coal. She remembered why she'd fallen in with him.

"Well?" Lloyd demanded, staring at her.

Suze quickly remembered that she had asked him a question.

"How much did we get?" Her southern voice wasn't lilting, but low and breathy, the kind she'd found men liked whispering in their ears.

"About sixteen thousand dollars."

Suzanna's face spread into a smile, her eyes lit with excitement. "Sixteen thousand dollars?"

"Give or take a thousand. Also some in change and jewelry," Robinson said. "Could have had more, but we didn't have time to pick up the pieces." The man turned to Suzanna. "Hi, Suze," he grinned at her, stroking the short beard that covered his chin but left his cheeks and jaw bare. "Feel like goin' swimmin'?"

"Not now, Steve." She shook off the thought of

14

physical contact with the man—Steve Robinson was greasy, pudgy, smelled bad and looked worse.

"Come on, you're a rich woman now." He grinned lasciviously and touched her shoulder.

Suzanna wrenched away from his hand. Sixteen thousand dollars! She breathed deeply. Even her father hadn't talked about that much money at one time.

Robinson's grin faded. "You shoulda been there, Suzanne. It was exciting. Real exciting. Wasn't it, Willis?"

The boy nodded, his face still flushed with the intensity of the new experience.

"I bet you would have loved to have blown those safes," Robinson said to the woman.

Suzanna turned to Lloyd. "What about next time? Can I?"

"What are you talking about?" Lloyd unstrapped the saddle bags and he walked to the mine.

"Damn you, Ray Lloyd!" Suzanna followed him. "You know what I'm asking! It's the same damn thing I always ask, day or night!"

"You want to help out on a job," Lloyd said flatly.

"That's right," Suzanna said.

"No shit?" Robinson said as he passed her.

Frustrated, Suzanna caught Lloyd's arm. "Come on, Ray. You know I'm as good a shot as Willis or even Robinson. You know I can ride and—"

"Watch that kind of talk, woman! No girl's a better shot than Stephen B. Robinson!"

"Maybe next time," Lloyd said and pulled her hand from his arm.

"That's what you said the last time! I'm tired of hearing that. I want to help you rob a train!"

The men laughed.

Suzanna turned crimson as they reached the mine. She ran inside and went to her bed—three blankets laid on the bare earth. She was furious, but didn't want Lloyd to see it. He'd think she was overly emotional, womanly. Yes, I'm a woman, she thought, but not a helpless weakling like Lloyd thinks I am. I've proven myself to him over and over. I can ride and shoot as well as any man, better than some. But all Ray, Steve or even Chuck see when they look at me are a pair of breasts or a furry crotch. Damn them! Damn all men!

"Suze?"

She looked up as her sister approached, a spatterware colander in her hands.

Suzanna cooled her anger. "Hello, Phoebe."

"Everything go fine?"

"Yes. I guess so. They got sixteen thousand."

Phoebe's lips parted in surprise.

"Damn it, Phoebe. I should have been able to go with them. Why do we have anything to do with men?"

Phoebe laughed. "Of all woman, you should know the answer, Suze. If we want to get money, we have to get it from men."

"Maybe so. I don't know."

"Lloyd's not going to change," she said in her sweet voice. She stroked her sister's hair as she sat beside her, the colander in her lap. "You shouldn't let him upset you."

"I don't want to talk about it," she said, shrugging off the feelings. "I'm sure you're bored hearing me complain about him."

Phoebe smiled, her skin glowing in the muted sunlight like porcelain. Her features were fragile, almost delicate; a barely-there chin, huge round eyes, small, tight red lips and high cheekbones. Softly red hair stood in curls on her head. Phoebe seemed a soap bubble, Suzanne thought, looking at her. If she touched her, Phoebe would break and vanish.

"I thought you were in love with Ray." Phoebe laid down the colander.

"I—that was a long time ago—six months, maybe? And I wasn't in love with *him*, just with what he did. A train robber. How romantic to a girl from Texas!"

Phoebe smirked. "I wouldn't call it romantic—he gets a black face from dynamite, bullet holes through his body, he's always glancing over his shoulder, and he has thousands of people wishing he was dead!" Phoebe's voice was astonishingly sweet, no matter what words she used.

"Yes, but let a train robber like Ray wrap his arms around me in the moonlight, then pull my body to his . . ." She sighed. "But that's in the past. Now I'm only here for the money."

Footsteps echoed in the mine as Robinson entered. He ignored Suzanna and looked at Phoebe.

"You wanna go swimmin'?" he asked.

"I don't understand what it is about train robbing that makes you want to screw so much," Suzanne said before Phoebe could respond.

He pretended not to see Suzanna. "So, Phoebe. You wanna?"

"I've—I've got some herbs to collect," she said at last, then threw Suze a fast smile.

"Great!" Robinson said. "I'll help you."

"Okay, but only if you let me work."

Robinson squeezed his crotch. "You can work on this."

Phoebe giggled excitedly, then glanced at Suze. Her sister's face had darkened considerably.

"Come on," Robinson said, pulling Phoebe off the bed and to her feet. They left the mine.

Suzanna sat on her bed and sighed. She'd left a house, a family, a rich husband—for what? A cold mine, three wild men, and tons of money she never saw.

Damn that Lloyd! Whatever he thinks or whatever he wants, I'll either help him with a train robbery, or plan one and do it myself. A moment later Suzanna laughed. It was a stupid idea. All she knew about robbing trains was the little she'd heard from Lloyd. The man had connections—he knew when payrolls and special shipments of money would be coming in through the area by train. Who told him?

She knew she'd never do it without Lloyd's help, and he wouldn't let her help him.

Lloyd walked into the cave, saw Suzanna sitting on her bed, then turned and left.

Damn him!

CHAPTER TWO

Spur McCoy touched the woman's shoulder tentatively and felt her pull back. She was nineteen, brown-haired, dressed as demurely as a schoolmarm in her simple black tight waisted dress that buttoned up to her neck, which was shrouded in a high, stiff collar of black material.

But below the collar her breasts surged out in perfect mounds, then her body tapered down to a narrow waist and flared out into feminine hips. She smiled seductively at Spur and blinked a few times, her pure white face relaxed and unselfconscious.

She was playing a game with McCoy as they stood in his Denver hotel room.

"Do you know what I don't like about you?" Karla purred, moving closer to him.

"No. What?" Spur was amused by the question.

"Guess."

"I've got a better plan. Tell me what you *do* like."

She looked him over, her smile broadening. "I like six foot two inches of hard muscles, reddish-brown hair, a thick moustache and muttonchop sideburns," she said, touching Spur at the appropriate places, "—powerful arms, flat stomach, and this." She laid her hand on his hardening groin.

Spur bent to kiss her head, but she moved away.

"Damnit, what *don't* you like?" he asked, almost irritated.

"Your style."

He stepped back. "My *what?*"

Karla's smile faded, then grew into an intense expression of hunger. "You treat me like a lady. I don't want that. Spur McCoy, I want you to throw me onto your hard bed, strip me naked, and push it in!"

He didn't have to be told twice. Spur lifted her from the floor and carried her to the bed across the room, then flung her down on it so hard she bounced twice—and giggled.

"Yes!"

As Spur pulled apart buttons and holes, unlaced and unhooked her various outer and undergarments, her face flushed. Karla's body shook slightly whenever Spur's fingers met her bare flesh, and she opened and closed her legs in anticipation, pressing her thighs together as he undressed her.

Spur wiped sweat from his forehead and pulled off her last garter, then peeled down the black silk stocking. He spread her legs wide and she groaned in need.

Staring at her exposed groin, Spur hurriedly threw off his boots and shirt, pants and underdrawers and fell on top of the squirming woman. He grasped her ankles and nudged his penis into position, spread her legs even further, holding them parallel with his body, then pushed into her.

Karla's back arched, thrusting out her pink nippled breasts as Spur hit home within her. He paused a moment, motionless, then reared back.

"Talk to me," Karla sighed. "Tell me what you're doing to my body."

Spur pumped back into her incredible warmth and tightness, holding her legs splayed, his hips setting up a fast tempo—one which he knew he could never maintain without losing control.

"I'm fucking you," he said, "ramming my cock in and out of your cunt."

She laughed low, filthily, pushing up to meet his thrusts to momentarily entwine their pubic hairs.

"Fuck me," Karla's voice had dropped a few notes. "Fuck my pussy. Jesus!"

Spur slowed his rhythm slightly, emphasizing the thrust, then the withdrawal, making Karla jump on the bed. Finally he pulled completely out, then rammed back into her anew with each thrust.

"Damn—damn!" Spur said, incredible sensations racing through his body. "You're so tight, Karla. Christ, you're driving me out of my mind!"

"God, I know. I know!"

Spur dropped her legs and, gripping her buttocks, pulled Karla's lower body off the bed, then punctuated his penetrations by jerking Karla toward him.

"You're so damned hot!" Spur said. "You're drinking my cock in. Jesus, Karla!" He looked down and watched himself driving into her, then glanced up at her bouncing breasts.

"Fuck me! Harder!" she said, nearly screaming.

Spur complied, pounding into her, finally dropping her back onto the bed, his body following hers, not missing a stroke. The bed shook and complained as he worked out his built-up, uncontrollable sexual desires with Karla, taking her just the way she told him to—in primal, animal lust.

"God! Oh God!" Karla shivered, her body shook and her eyes screwed shut as his penis touched off an explosion between her legs, sending her into ecstasy. Her hands gripped his waist, rearing back onto him, grinding her groin into his as she shook through her orgasm.

The woman's pleasure touched off Spur's, and he felt the first strainings deep within him. He worked furiously, sweat dripping from his forehead, chest and armpits onto Karla's body, lathering her as he prepared to ejaculate.

"God! Oh God!" she moaned. "Come inside me! Shoot it, Spur! Now!"

He groaned in agony, his hips a blur and his thrusts growing in intensity. Spur rocked back and forth as, for ten dizzying seconds, he emptied himself into her, pounding so hard Karla's face contracted with each inward push.

"Jesus Christ!" she said, pulling him down on top of her as his orgasm ended.

They lay panting, their slick bodies fused together.

"Nothing's better than a good, hard fuck from a man who knows what he's doing," she said, panting, "and who's got something to do it with!"

He blew hot breath against her ear, unable to respond to her comment, waiting for the ringing in his ears to cease and leave him in peace.

Karla's tongue snaked out and licked Spur's hot neck, tasting his sweaty flesh, and he shivered.

"Stop that!" he managed to gasp.

Karla frowned and wrapped her legs around his. "All right. I just wanted to taste you."

"I'm just—it's just that—" (Pant, pant.)

"I know," she said, dreamily. "So am I. God, what a rod you've got on you! I've seen my share and you've been blessed! I feel like you've driven me to heaven and back with that thing!" She squeezed around him to emphasize her point.

Spur yelped and raised himself halfway off her, not breaking their intimate connection. Karla laughed at his expression of pain mixed with pleasure.

"Okay. I'll stop torturing you. I just wanted you to know that I appreciate it."

"Sure. No problem," he said. "Now, if the room'll stop spinning, I'll be fine."

She laughed and kissed his neck as a knock sounded loudly through Spur's hotel room.

"Damn." He pulled out of her, lifted himself from the bed, threw a blanket over Karla, stepped into his discarded pants, and pulled them up as he walked to the door. Spur opened it just as he finished buttoning.

"What?" he asked, with such force the knocker stepped back two feet.

"You—you tole me to come here if a wire came in for you," the young boy said, standing clutching an envelope and wearing an oversized hat.

Spur remembered. He'd gone to the Western Union office and found the boy loafing around—he was the son of the Western Union man. Spur told him to bring any wires that came in for him—he was expecting a new assignment any day and wanted to know the *bad news* as soon as possible.

23

"Remember?" the kid said.

"Yeah. Got something for me?"

"Sure." He handed Spur the wire.

McCoy smiled and found a quarter in his pocket, flipped it to the boy, and shut the door.

"Thanks, mister!" he said before it slammed.

Spur turned back and pulled off his pants, stepped out of them, then sat naked beside Karla on the bed. She threw back the blanket.

"What's that?" she asked, snuggling up next to him on her knees.

"A wire, from a friend." He sat with it, unopened, in his hand.

The woman pushed her warm breasts against his shoulder. "Aren't you going to read it?"

"Later," he said, not wanting to share its news with the woman. Spur didn't know who she really was or what kind of friends she had. He'd seen her on the street, talked to her, and she'd invited herself to his room.

"Look, it was great," Spur said.

"No you don't, Spur!" she said. "You're not getting rid of me that easily! Look at these!" She cupped her breasts, pointing them at Spur's mouth. "Don't they look tasty? You forgot them earlier."

"Didn't forget," Spur said, gazing at the huge globes. "Just couldn't reach them." He moved his head forward and licked her right nipple, then took the breast in his mouth, sucking it in like an infant.

He then switched to its twin, covering the quarter-sized areola with his mouth and making the nipple stand up firm. While he worked over her breasts Spur kept the wire tightly clamped in one hand. Though his attention was turned away from its momentarily, he hadn't forgotten it.

"That's it!" she said. "Yes!"

Spur chewed on the breast, and he felt her pressing him down backward on the bed. She knelt over him, then pushed her breasts into his face. He chewed and sucked, licked and ate to his satisfaction.

Karla moved down alongside him until her mouth closed in on his penis. She sucked in the head, squeezing it between her lips, tonguing him, then slid down until Spur felt himself enter her throat. he gasped at the sensation.

Karla sucked him with enthusiasm and not more than a minute or two later Spur spurted deep in her throat. He slammed his body against the bed, revelling in the intense pleasure Karla's mouth produced. She drained the last drops and then lifted her head.

"Nice," she said, her eyes sparkling.

Spur gasped in answer.

Two hours later, she was gone. Spur had escorted Karla to a restaurant; it turned out she was in Denver for the day, before taking a train east that night. After she had left, Spur went back to his hotel room and opened the wire.

In moments his new assignment unfolded: The Union Pacific railroad company had contacted General Halleck in Washington for help. The wire read:

"A gang of three, possibly four have period-ically—at least once or twice a month for the past four months—robbed Union Pacific trains, primarily on a stretch of track near Pardo, Wyoming Territory. $200,000 in gold double eagles will be shipped from the New Badham & Badham bank back east to a bank in Sacramento. Your assignment is to protect the gold and locate the robbers. The shipment will pass through Wyoming territory on April 20th."

Spur sighed. Wyoming territory—lots of land, little of anything else.

The telegram also stated that Silas Fredrickson, president of the Union Pacific, would arrive in Cheyenne the following day to talk with Spur, bringing with him a special *security coordinator* to help in the matter. Spur frowned as he tore up the wire. He worked alone, and didn't need anyone to tell him what to do.

He'd have to work around the problem. Spur dressed in his working clothes—a dark blue business suit, black vest, tie and boots, a white shirt with a stiff blue collar, and a black hat. Might as well go to Cheyenne and use it as a working base for starters, Spur thought, and then go wherever necessary to find the robbers.

Spur McCoy wasn't an ordinary man kicking around the west, looking for adventure. His father was a well-known merchant and trader in New York City. Spur was raised and educated in New York, attended Harvard and graduated in 1858. After two years with his father's firm, Spur joined the Union Army with a commission as second lieutenant. He had advanced to captain.

After two years of army life he went to Washington, D.C. as aide to senator Arthur B. Walton of New York, a long time family friend.

In the 1860's Congress became aware of a need for a federal law enforcement group to protect the currency from counterfeiting. Congress put together a law creating the United States Secret Service in 1865. Later its duties were expanded to cover any crime where the perpatrators crossed state or territorial lines.

Gradually, the Secret Service had to do other federal business, since they were the only agency with enforcement personnel. Quickly, the men of the Secret Service were handling a wide range of law enforcement problems, including counterfeiting.

Spur joined the service as one of its first members and served six months in the Washington office. He was then transferred to the St. Louis branch and was assigned to handle all cases west of the Mississippi. He was chosen from ten men because he was the best horseback rider and had won the service pistol marksmanship contest. The government considered both of these attributes of the utmost importance in the western region, where law had frequently only recently settled in.

Spur's immediate superior, General Wilton D. Halleck, U.S. Army (retired), worked in the Washington, D.C. headquarters and was second in command of the service.

So far, the Secret Service had lost six men, all shot to death in the performance of their duties. Being a Secret Service man was a dangerous job.

Spur McCoy had no close connections, no sweetheart or home town roots, and enjoyed his life. He also made damn sure he wasn't the seventh man killed in the line of duty.

Spur packed his bag and carried it and his Spencer rifle with him as he left. He paid at the hotel's front desk and set off for the train station. He had an hour or so to wait.

The bustle on the streets of Denver would be in sharp contrast with the emptiness, the flat high plains and mountains that awaited him in Wyoming territory. The change suited him fine. There were too many people in Denver, too many problems, too much noise. Spur enjoyed the open country of the west almost as much as he did the company of women.

Then Spur brought himself back to reality. He'd be working the trains, at least part of the time. No sleeping under the stars, no fragrant campfires crackling him to sleep or wild bird calls to wake him as the sun dazzled the eastern edge of the world. Instead, it would be Pullmans and club cars.

Hell. He'd try to hold up under the strain!

CHAPTER THREE

"I've changed my mind," Silas Fredrickson said, slamming his fist onto the oak table and staring at his daughter. "You're not going!"

"Father!" Helena gasped. "You can't mean that!"

The short, rounded, well dressed man with an open, fleshy face stabbed an unlit cigar in the air. "You can't change my mind, so don't try."

"But I'm already packed! I've got three trunks full of dresses and corsets and stocking and hats and—"

"I don't care. You're behaving like an irresponsible child. You can't handle the position," Silas Fredrickson said, shaking his head. "You had me talked into this crazy idea of yours yesterday, but no longer."

Helena tucked a wisp of blonde hair back into the attractive bun on her head and calmed her face. "That's not fair. You haven't let me try! If I have to sit home all day for the rest of my life I'll die of boredom, an old maid with no life to look back on."

"I'd hardly call you an old maid," he said, smiling.

She moved to her father, her aristocratic face poised, the chin held slightly lower than usual. Helena placed her hands on his well padded shoulders. "Father, give me a chance. Help me to prove I'm capable of doing *something*. I can't sew, I can't cook, I can't even keep house—not that the servants have given me the opportunity to try. Please, father!" Her eyes locked with his momentarily.

Silas sighed. "Too much is at stake here for you to act childish." He hesitated. "All right," he said, sighing. "You can go ahead and work with security. But don't get in the man's way if the train *is* robbed. Just keep your pretty head down and don't move."

"Thank you. I will!" She kissed his cheek and looked at him, beaming.

Silas Fredrickson smiled. "Not let me get back to work. Aren't you going to Minnie's for tea?"

Her hand flew to her mouth. "Oh dear! I completely forgot. Bye, father!"

He mumbled an answer as she raced from his study. She had the knack of talking him into doing exactly what she wanted, no matter how hard he protested.

Helena Fredrickson was a woman who knew what she wanted, he thought wearily, then returned to his paperwork.

Ray Lloyd buttoned up his fly and stepped from the bushes toward the mine's entrance. Rich, hearty steam rose from a cauldron hanging over the small fire, shielded from sight by a mass of boulders and rocks directly opposite the mine's entrance. Phoebe

Buckland stirred the thick stew while bending over, thrusting out her rear. She smiled at him, then turned back to her work.

Lloyd sighed. Nothing he liked better than a woman with a good behind. It was the top half of a woman that usually got him into trouble. Thinking about it as he squatted by the fire, warming his hands in the thickening dusk, Lloyd couldn't remember why he'd let the sisters join his gang, even as lesser members who didn't actually participate in the robberies. Whatever gave him that stupid idea?

Then he remembered the first time he'd seen Suzanna Buckland—her body tightly wrapped in a thin layer of fine fabric, the face of an angel peering at him in a strange combination of terror and arousal.

Ray Lloyd and Steve Robinson had barged into a train's day car and demanded that the passengers turn over their money and valuables. As he stared down at Suzanna, she willingly handed her purse and money to him, but didn't meet his eyes. The younger woman seated to her right stared at him in fright. Seconds later, after he'd moved to the next row of seats, Lloyd realized that the woman had stared at his crotch, her lips parted, breathing heavily.

She'd been excited during the robbery. When he'd finished the car, he glanced back at her—but her seat was empty. The woman and her companion, whoever she had been, were gone.

"Where'd they go?" he'd yelled at Robinson, who turned back to him and shrugged.

Cursing, they'd left the train with their meager take—Lloyd knew there was nothing of value in the express car—and ran to their horses, fending off the firemen and brakemen. The two men stopped short and stared up at the women from the train mounted on their horses—next to an astonished Chuck Willis.

"They said you asked them along," Willis had explained.

Faced with the wasted seconds of explanation and the hiss of the train's brakes, Lloyd and Robinson slid up behind the two women on their horses and rode hard away from the tracks.

"You have some explaining to do, bitch," he had yelled into Suzanna's ear. If she had responded, he hadn't heard it. By the time they made it safely into the endless foothills that snuggled up to the Rocky Mountains, Lloyd couldn't slap down the tremendous erection that sliding against Suzanna's warm rump had produced.

After a few minutes of negotiations, Suzanna and her younger sister Phoebe were allowed to stay— provided they looked after meals and didn't mind sharing their beds with the men occasionally.

Now it had been three months, and Lloyd was tiring of them. Suzanna nagged him until he wanted to punch her—she'd gotten this crazy idea that she could *help him out*. He smiled at the thought. As far as he was concerned, she helped him every time she spread her legs or knelt before him.

But she did have spirit, and Lloyd liked that. Phoebe was almost boringly sweet in comparison— gentle, kind with a delicate beauty that seemed destined to be destroyed by nature. Neither was a virgin, and hadn't acted like one. Lloyd admitted it was pleasant having someone else to look at besides Robinson and Willis. Before the women came, life was boring and frustrating.

Lloyd was startled back to the present as Phoebe moved off in search of some forgotten ingredient. He rubbed his palms together, generating more warmth. The flames slowly increased in brilliance as the dusk dragged on.

A high scream pierced the calm moment, sending Lloyd to his feet. It had come from behind him—from the mine.

Birds flapped noisily overhead, disturbed by the cry, as Lloyd ran inside. Phoebe sat rigid, her hand pressed against the mine's uneven floor.

"Phoebe, you goddamned idiot! I thought you were getting shot or raped or something!"

"Don't move!" she said, her voice strained.

"Why the hell not?" he thundered back.

"Don't! I was getting some potatoes and a scorpion crawled onto my hand." Breath puffed gently from her cheeks. "It hasn't moved since it climbed up on me. Ray, what should I do?"

"Don't do anything," he said, approaching her cautiously.

The scorpion lifted its tail in anger, stinger poised for a vicious attack, and inched up Phoebe's trembling arm. Lloyd grabbed a corner of the blanket lying on top of a wooden box of supplies, letting it unfold as he dragged it behind him.

"When I tell you to, jerk your hand toward you as fast as you can—but not before I tell you." Damn fool woman, he thought.

Phoebe's face was slick with fear, her eyes shut. She seemed to be mumbling some sort of prayer. Lloyd moved to within two feet of her. The scorpion had travelled up to Phoebe's elbow, and its sharp feet gripped her flesh to climb.

"Ray, I—I can't hold back much longer," she whispered.

Lloyd suddenly sprang. "Now!" he shouted, slapping the blanket toward her arm.

Phoebe pulled it violently in toward her, perfectly timed so that the blanket knocked the scorpion off her arm and onto the ground. Lloyd stamped the blanket with his feet, then cautiously pulled it up. The trampled scorpion had lost its legs and the tail lay venomously poised, but twisted into strange angles. He ground it into the earth and heaped rocks on top of it.

"You all right?" he asked, turning his attention back to the woman.

Phoebe sighed and placed her hand to her throat. "Yes. I'm fine." She brushed her arm a few times, unconsciously trying to remove the now deceased arachnid.

Lloyd nodded and stood. "Be careful where you stick you hands."

"I know; I just didn't look."

He left the mine as Suzanna rushed past him to go to Phoebe. Life sure would be boring without the women, Lloyd confessed to himself. But he'd gotten along without them before, and he could do it again.

He'd made his decision. The women left in two weeks—whether they like it or not.

No sense in spoiling the next fourteen days, though—he'd wait and tell them a few days before. That way they'll still have time to get ready to go—and they also wouldn't withhold their favors when he felt the urge.

Suzanna listened to her sister's peaceful breathing

34

as she lay on the fairly soft stack of Indian blankets in the mine. She shivered and pulled the covers higher around her neck. If it hadn't been April, she'd swear it was growing colder each night.

Suzanna Buckland had married a wealthy cattleman in Dallas, Texas two years ago, and had a carefree life of endless parties and teas and barbecues. But at night, when the guests had left and she was alone with her wealthy husband, she bore the brunt of his wrath. If she'd really had the lovers her husband accused her of having they would have seen the bruises on her breasts, back and thighs. He'd beaten her whenever he felt the need—to him, violence was a substitute for sex. He was gentle in bed, but nowhere else.

One day four months ago Suzanna had had enough. She went to her bank, drew out five hundred dollars, and took her carriage across town to see her sister. Phoebe had lived with their parents since the death of her husband in the war.

Suzanna quickly told her sister what she'd done, and the two decided to leave that night. Eight hours later they were on the train north to Omaha, then transferred west on the way to California. On that trip she'd met Ray Lloyd and Steve Robinson, liked what she saw, and suddenly changed her plans. Sacramento or San Francisco would have to wait.

She was beyond caring that she slept with three different men, or that she shared them with her sister. It was a simple, practical way of living. She never let any of the men penetrate her when she wasn't in the mood. But the dark good looks and powerful frame of Ray Lloyd often helped her warm up to his advances.

He was a strange man, Suzanna thought as she lay

sleepless, listening to Robinson wander around outside and then move to the fire. Ray Lloyd slept with her, kissed her as passionately as any man, but he seemed cold, empty. Maybe there wasn't much more to him than what she'd seen—an egotistical, overbearing, train robbing man's man.

But he was a means to an end, she resolved. Soon she and Phoebe would leave the men behind, when Lloyd gave them the money he owed them. Suzanna had managed to keep the nearly five hundred dollars she'd brought with her a secret; not even Phoebe knew the exact amount. But Lloyd had promised them a tenth of the money they earned from robberies to split between them. She hadn't seen a penny of it so far.

Suzanna wasn't worried about that. If she had to leave with Phoebe in the night she would. But the thought of all those dollars had made her hesitate about heading on further west more than once. She simply couldn't turn down that much money, which had to amount to thousands of dollars by now. He'd taken in sixteen thousand dollars on the last job alone!

It was hidden in various places, and deposited in a string of banks under various names. Lloyd didn't keep any of the loot in the mine itself. He had his records with one or two men. Suzanna wondered if even Lloyd knew how much money he had stashed away.

If he didn't know, he could be losing some of it— some of his *friends* might have already taken all they had and left him high and dry. If she could just get the names and locations of some of the banks, perhaps she could pose as his wife and withdraw some of the money.

36

No. It would be too difficult to convince them—she had no papers, no proof. And she couldn't think how to forge them. She frowned. Now that her mind was fully occupied with the problem, Suzanna knew she wouldn't sleep that night. She might as well make use of the time with creative thinking.

If she could find out the name of one of the town men, perhaps she could persuade him to split the money with her, and they'd go off to Europe, or New York. Or, perhaps she could simply talk Steve Robinson or Chuck Willis into revealing the sites of the money he'd buried—surely they knew. The men had helped him dig a few times.

Suzanna frowned and turned on her stomach, pressing her body against the earth. Dreaming wouldn't accomplish anything, she told herself. If she wasn't careful she'd be trapped under Lloyd's power. As much as she bothered him about participating in a robbery, Suzanna didn't see herself as an outlaw woman. She didn't have the heart for it. She missed four walls around her, a ceiling overhead, soft clothing and fancy parties.

Suzanna dismissed the thoughts. She had given that up months ago. Now she'd have to wait a while longer to get back to the easy life, and she'd do it without a husband to beat her between cattle shows and balls on her own, with as much money as she wanted.

She'd already spent far too much time out here in the wilderness with Ray Lloyd and the others—in fact, she'd only planned to be with them for a week at the most. Suzanna felt if she didn't leave soon she never would.

But soon she'd be rich and back in civilization.

The dreams crystallized in her mind as Suzanna closed her eyes, rolled her head to the right, and slipped into the blackness of sleep.

Next to her, Phoebe stirred, her face tense. She brushed her arm blindly, her nails scraping against the warm flannel of her nightgown. Still enwrapped in sleep, Phoebe's lips parted, arched, as if struggling to mouth a soundless word.

CHAPTER FOUR

Spur's trip to Cheyenne was uneventful. The Union Pacific's train #107 slid into Cheyenne's rustic station a little over ten hours after departing from Denver, good time on a track that often climbed several thousand feet, then dropped as many, in as little as ten miles.

Three-year old Cheyenne wasn't a town, Spur thought. Not yet. It had sprung up with the Union Pacific railroad construction crews reached that point. Unlike most of these sudden railroad towns, Cheyenne had taken root. As he left the train Spur saw that it had buildings, saloons, carriages and fights, but no hospital, town hall or jail. As Spur understood it, the last was in the works, and in a year or two they should have a place to lock up their bad—and hopefully someone to do the job.

He walked down the muddy street looking for the Occidental Hotel, the one Halleck had directed him to. Silas Fredrickson was to meet him there at noon to discuss the railroad's problems.

Spur checked in, dropped his rifle and bag in his second floor room, locked the door and struck out to look over Cheyenne. The men and women on its streets were as raw as the town, upstarts transplanted from back east living in a town whose name was nearly longer than its history. Spur could feel the spirit of the community that lived on the edge of civilization, and it wasn't a friendly one.

He stepped into the Excellent Saloon and wended his way through the smoke-filled room to the bar, where he ordered a warm beer. With two hours to kill, Spur might as well slake his thirst and enjoy himself. After a few minutes he got caught up in a game of faro. He lost ten dollars but enjoyed himself.

At ten till noon Spur returned to his fairly plush room at the Occidental and stood looking out the half-curtained second floor window down on Cheyenne. He was surprised by an insistent knocking on the door.

Spur opened it and saw a short, round man with an elegant, reserved woman standing beside him.

"Can I help you?" Spur asked suspiciously.

"Mr. McCoy?"

"Yes."

"I'm Silas Fredrickson," he said, extending his hand. The two men shook. "This is my daughter, Helena." He ended the shake and looked at her.

"How do you do, ma'am," Spur said, showing his approval with a smile. He bent and kissed the hand she offered him, then released it and looked behind them.

"Were you expecting someone else?" Silas Fredrickson asked, surprised.

"Please come in," Spur said, moving back to

allow their entrance to his room. "I thought General Halleck's telegram mentioned a security coordinator," Spur said as they moved to the overstuffed couches near the paned windows.

Helena started slightly, but Silas slid his hand over hers as he sat beside her.

"And so it did. Helena has that position."

She stared fiercely at Spur. She's testing me, he thought, judging my reaction to the news. Spur didn't conceal his surprise.

"I know, I know, I'm a woman," Helena said before Spur could respond. "But I can do the job. Just give me a fair chance. That's all I ask." Her voice was controlled, but Spur saw what he felt was unjustified anger. He hadn't said anything yet.

"Miss Fredrickson, don't get the idea that I don't approve, or think you incapable. I was simply surprised to find a woman, as any man would be."

"There, there, Helena," Silas said. "We've come all this way and you're not going to spoil things. I want you to work together as friends."

She steeled herself but didn't speak.

"So, on to work," Fredrickson said. "We desperately need your help. We've lost over $150,000 in the last six months from train robberies. We don't know if they're connected, but those in the Wyoming Territory seem to be the work of one group. With the $200,000 gold shipment on the 20th, we need a miracle to keep our losses from doubling over-night."

"And you called *him?*" Helena asked amusedly.

Spur felt the challenge. "Miss Fredrickson, I don't claim to be divine, simply good at what I do. I'll find the gang that's been robbing your trains." His gaze bored into hers until she had to turn her head.

"Helena, really!" Silas Fredrickson said. "Behave yourself or I'll send you back home!"

She rose abruptly. "Excuse me," she said, crossing to the hall door. She left the room.

Her father shrugged. "She's a strong-minded woman. I don't claim to control her."

"Will she be a problem?"

"How?"

Spur shrugged. "I don't let anything get in my way when I work. If I trip over her every time I turn around—" Spur felt the anger rising in him and forced it down.

"I know, I know," Fredrickson said, removing a cigar from his vest pocket and a match. "Would you like one?"

"No thanks."

Fredrickson lit the fragrant tobacco cylinder and sucked at its tip, then blew out rum scented clouds of blue smoke.

"You don't have to tell me how you feel about her, but let's give her the opportunity to prove herself."

"Why did you ever let her tag along in the first—never mind," Spur said, shaking his head. "Doesn't matter now. I'll get the job done whether she's around or not. She won't bother me."

Silas brightened. "Good. Now, to business. We don't have a clear description of the men, but there is a woman who might—Agatha Taylor. She lives in Dolmen, a town down the line west, on Oak Street. She might be a good place to start looking."

"Has she been questioned before?" Spur asked.

Silas shook his head. "She's been out west, and

only returned home three days ago. She wired the Union Pacific saying she was present during a robbery and if we wanted her help, we should call on her.''

Spur nodded. ''What about your train detectives? Have they come up with anything?''

''Not much. The last robbery they found footprints alongside the tracks, followed them for a few hundred feet, then lost them in a mass of hoofprints. Then it started to pour down rain, washing out the evidence. Other robberies have turned out about the same—no leads.''

''What about local businesses, ranches, general stores? The robbers have to eat, buy ammunition, dynamite and other supplies.''

''We've checked thoroughly, and haven't found a thing. The men may have paid someone to keep quiet, or they may have a town man working with them.'' He shook his head again. ''We're counting on you. If you can find them before the 20th, all the better. If not—''

''There's no way the shipment can be delayed, or the date of departure changed?''

Fredrickson puffed and shook his head. ''No.''

Spur frowned.

''Most of the robberies have occured in the same general type of location—a long way from the nearest settlement, usually while climbing a steep grade, when the train slows down from its 35 to 40 miles per hour speed. Sometimes only the passengers are robbed, or the express car is broken into. Sometimes both. We've got only one of the bastard robbers so far —a guy who tried to do it alone. He entered a passenger car and demanded their money, only to be shot dead by two men behind him as they independently stood and fired.''

''Can't you hire a detective for each car?''

''Sure,'' he said. ''In fact, we did, for a new trial run. But the detectives simply got disarmed or killed and the trains were robbed anyway. It's getting harder to hire good men; a lot of the *romance of the rails* is fading.'' He drew on the cigar again. ''If this keeps up, we'll be ruined. Ticket sales are down from what they were six months ago. Some big-shot eastern writer happened to be riding a train that was robbed, and, even though he never saw the men he wrote up a complete, detailed article describing the incident. The day that edition was on the streets our east coast ticket offices suffered a twenty-five percent decrease in sales.''

''I see,'' Spur said.

''You're my last hope,'' Silas said simply, flicking his ashes into the lead tray on the table. ''Mine—and the Union Pacific's.''

Suzanna found him with the horses, pouring water into their troughs from a stream filled bucket. The horses stood contented, tethered, shifting from the water to the mounds of wild hay that the men collected to feed them.

''Hello,'' Suzanna said.

Lloyd looked at her and nodded in reply.

Undaunted, she went on. ''I want the ten percent of the money you owe Phoebe and me.'' Her soft Texan accent rang clear and sweet as she stood before him in a leather skirt, checkered blouse and boots, a Stetson firmly parked on her head.

Lloyd set the bucket down and laughed. "You want what?"

Suzanna's cheeks burned in spite of her resolve. "You heard me! I'm not joking!"

"Convince me.' Lloyd laughed from his hard belly, shaking his body.

"Listen to me, goddamn it!" Suzanna said. "I'm tired of you and Steve and Chuck pawing me all the time, never leaving me alone! You even spy on me when I go to relieve myself—don't think I don't know that!" Her voice vibrated with rage, cheeks shining scarlet in the morning sun. "I'm tired of the way you treat me because—"

"You're a woman!" Lloyd grew sedate but grinned. "Shit! How could I ever forget you're a woman?'

"Stop that!" she drawled. "Stop trying to change the subject!" Suzanna grabbed his left arm and shook it. "And I'm especially tired of being left behind with these goddamned horses! Do you know what it's like to stand around for four horses, feeling like you're the fifth? Knowing you're having all that excitement while I itch to get out there with you?"

"You make my heart bleed."

"I know why you won't let me help out with the robberies. Then you'd really have to give me my share of the money. That's it, isn't it? Well, I'm tired of your empty promises. I want my money!"

"Cut the crap, woman," Lloyd said. He kicked the bucket and twisted his arms to grip her wrists, then pulled her to him. "Come here. Come here and find out if *I'm* tired of *you!*" He smiled as Suzanna struggled, digging her heels into the earth.

The horses knickered, spooked by the woman's violent actions and screams.

"Goddamn it, calm down!" Lloyd jerked her towards him, enjoying the sight of her breasts bouncing before him. "You want some excitement? Come on, *girl*. Yes, little girl. I've got all the excitement you need hanging right here." He thrust his groin lewdly toward her.

"Leave me alone!" Suzanna screamed. Tapping every ounce of strength she willed herself to kick hard straight up. Her boot toe banged into Lloyd's right arm, forcing the elbow to bend suddenly. She found her left arm free and slapped his cheek, simultaneously pushing her foot against his chest.

Lloyd stumbled back, dazed at the woman's vicious, sudden attack.

"You fucking bitch!" he said, lunging.

Suzanna, now free, ran from the horses into the dense growth of pines, firs and aspens. She found an ancient pine with a truck that spanned several feet, secreted herself behind it, then looked up at the tree. Branches jutted out from the trunk at just the right angles. If she could reach them . . .

She climbed the tree, forcing herself not to look down as she inched along its truck. The leather skirt scraped against the gnarled bark. Finally she came to a massive limb with a natural hollow and scrambled into it, then fitted her bottom into the depression and drew her knees up.

Suzanna didn't look down, but she was startled when the distant crunching steps passed directly beneath her—then stopped. She shut her eyes and prayed to any god that would listen for ten seconds, then sighed as the steps resumed, leading off to her right.

She congratulated herself, then noticed the incredible surges of power flowing through her body. She felt strong, poised, confident of herself for the first time since she'd been married. That damned Lloyd couldn't always have his way with her. She smiled, remembering his reaction to her attack. He'd never think of her as only a weak female again.

But as she sat in the tree, unwilling to leave its security and half afraid to make a descent, Suzanna's triumph faded. What had her actions cost her? Now she and Phoebe definitely had to leave, with no chance of getting the money Lloyd owed them.

She sighed, thinking of Phoebe. Sometimes Suzanna wished she'd never taken her sister along. Phoebe would have probably been promised to some rich man by now, happy and content with her simple life.

Then she shook her head. Phoebe's learning more about life in these months than she would if she were married again. It's good for her. And after they'd had their fun, seen all they could, Suzanna knew Phoebe would remarry.

That brought to mind her own marriage. As soon as she got to a city or town she'd wire the family attorney and tell him she was suing for divorce. She knew it would scandalize Dallas—and was glad of it.

Suzanna sat in the tree for hours, thinking, until she heard a faint rustling in the leaves below.

Lloyd, she thought, then a chill swept through her. It could be a mountain lion. Suzanna was suddenly aware of the danger. If it climbed up the tree after her, how much higher could she go?

Suzanna stared fearfully at the tree that stretched above her another thirty or forty feet, then down as the rustling became ordered, patterned footsteps. She almost sighed. Lloyd wasn't even trying to hide his approach, she thought, but realized he had no need.

She had nowhere to go.

CHAPTER FIVE

Spur McCoy walked into Young's General Store in Green River. The shop smelled of new cloth, sulphurous matches and tobacco, and was crammed with boxes and cans and jars that spilled over counters and onto the floor. The secret service man moved to the counter and waited.

A moment later a burly, whiskered man walked out of the curtained stock room, wiping his hands on the stained apron around his ample waist.

"Yeah?" he said.

"I'm Spur McCoy, working for the Union Pacific on the train robberies in this area."

"I see. Anything I can do for you to help?"

"Sure. You can answer some questions."

"I'll be glad to, but I already did—for another Union Pacific detective that was around here last week."

"Did anyone come in here buying a lot of supplies, including dynamite, regularly?"

The man spat on the floor. "Lots of people."

"Anyone who acted suspicious?"

"I don't know. Kind of hard to tell. I try to mind my own business, if you know what I mean—it's a good way to keep breathing." The man pressed his palms flat against the wooden counter surface. "Any more questions?"

Spur smiled while he studied the man. Did he know something, or was he just being careful?

"You know this isn't just for the railroad's benefit, Young. This will help everyone. If I don't find those train robbers the line's going to die. How'd you like to see Green River dry up and blow away with the next wind that whistles by?"

"I'd just move on to the next town," Young said, philosophically. "I'm sorry I can't help you out." He turned and walked back toward the stock room.

"Twenty dollars."

The man halted and turned. "Twenty dollars? For what?"

"Information." He stared hard at the man and detected a flicker of—something.

Young hesitated, furious thought working itself out in his skull, and for a moment Spur saw him relax and almost speak. Then he tensed up again—the veins stood out on his neck—and he shook his head.

"I don't know nothing."

"Forty." Spur took two double eagles from his pocket and laid them on the counter, where the gleamed in the sunshine that slanted in through the shop window. It was probably more profit than the store made in a month.

Young slowly stepped back to the counter, his eyes riveted on the coins. "You never saw me," he said. "You never came in here and talked with me. Right?"

"Right."

Young's tongue touched his lips as he reached for the coins. Spur slammed his hand down on top of them.

"First, tell me."

The shopkeeper glanced surreptitiously over his shoulders, then bent toward Spur. His voice wasn't much more than a whisper.

"A short, stocky man comes in here once, twice a month, buying ammunition. He says he sometimes can't get it where he usually goes. First time he told me not to tell anyone I'd seen him, and paid me double what the stuff was worth. The next time, he slipped me fifty dollars. *Fifty dollars!* Christ, I couldn't believe it." The man's voice was hushed, excited.

"What's he look like?"

"I don't know; I'm not the kind of guy that looks at other guys. Hell, he was shorter than me, skinnier, maybe black hair."

"Moustache?"

"Yeah."

"You know where he usually buys his ammunition when he doesn't come here?"

"Not sure. Hell, I think he said Pardo once."

"Where's that? Around here?"

Young nodded. "It's a new town near Rock Springs, just a piss-pool of a place. I think that's what he said. Kinda shut up right after that, like he'd said something he wasn't supposed to."

Spur lifted his hand from the counter. The fat man grabbed the gold and stuffed it in his cash drawer.

"Get on out of here!" Young said. "I never saw you, you never saw me."

"Right. Thanks." Spur exited the shop and walked out onto the muddy, bumpy street. He had a start. A black-haired, stocky, short man who bought ammunition from a shopkeeper in Green River. Not unusual, he thought. But one who paid the man to forget him—that was suspicious.

Spur headed on to his next stop, the Green River Hotel. Maybe the desk clerk had seen the man.

Oscar Young pulled open the cash drawer with its cash box and removed the two twenty dollar gold pieces. He looked at them, his eyes wide, and stuffed them into his pocket. He banged the drawer shut with his left hand as the front door opened. Young looked up—and felt his knees shake.

It was the man who'd paid him to keep quiet.

Young's stomach boiled up a wicked brew of fear as he looked at the man, trembling.

"Three boxes—" the man began.

"I didn't tell him anything!" Young blurted out.

The dark haired man broke off his sentence and sized up the shopkeeper.

"You what?"

Young stiffened. He couldn't control the trembling that wracked his body; his knees shook uncontrollably, sending the rest of his body into a frantic dance.

"Goddamn it!" the man said. "You mother-fucker!" He lunged over the counter and grabbed Young by the throat. "Who've you been talking to?"

"I—I—no one," Young choked out.

"Bullshit!" he said succinctly. "What'd you say?"

"Nothing! I swear it! Shit, I thought you were someone else!" Young continued to shake.

"You fuckin' bastard! After I pay you fifty you open your fat, ugly mouth and start talking!" He released the shopkeeper.

Young backed against the rear wall next to the door. "What—what are you going to do?"

The man drew his revolver, then thrust it smoothly back home. "Too noisy. But I know something a hell of a lot quieter." He produced a lethal six-inch blade, held it to Young's chin, then climbed over the counter. Once on the other side he lowered the knife and plunged it into the man's stomach.

It drove deep into bone and muscle and gristle, and he strained to push the blade deeper. Young's eyes glazed, his midsection suffering an uncontrollable spasm as his attacker savagely twisted the blade, then cut upward, ripping open Young's heart. The shopkeeper groaned and slumped to the floor behind the counter, dead.

The dark man slipped the knife from Young's body and wiped its blade on a flour sack lying against the counter. He stuffed the weapon into the sheath hanging from his belt, then helped himself to ten boxes of ammunition of various types and wrapped them up with paper and string. He casually glanced down at the body, shrugged and bent to search the man's pockets. He found two double eagles. Smiling, he pocketed them and walked quickly from the store, stepped into the saddle and headed out of town.

* * *

Spur sipped watered whiskey in the club car on the way to Dolmen, almost halfway between Cheyenne and Rock Springs. First he'd talk to the woman who'd witnessed the robbery.

Spur went to the address he'd received after arriving in Dolmen and knocked on the impressively built split-pine house. Few other homes appeared to have been built with such care in the small town; each board fitted snugly against the next; windows had been carefully framed, doors hung straight, and a fresh coat of white paint had recently been applied.

A few moments later a pinch-faced elderly woman, probably in her sixties Spur thought, opened the door a crack.

"Yes, young man?" she said in a steel-hard voice. Her white hair was elaborately knotted on her head, and tiny glasses perched on the woman's strong nose. She wore a simple black dress with puff sleeves that stretched from the bottom of her prominent chin to the floor.

"Agatha Taylor?" Spur asked.

"That's right." Suspicion shone in her eyes.

"I'm Spur McCoy, from the Union Pacific."

Her eyes lit at once. Instantly the frowning, sharp grandmother disappeared, and she smiled. "Yes, of course. You're here about the robbery. Come in."

Spur entered the well appointed home and smelled lavender and freshly brewed tea. He stood in the hall until she motioned him to follow her into the parlor.

Agatha bustled off and returned with a full tea tray which she sat on a table. "Now," she said, settling into a rocker and lifting the pot as Spur sat,

"Let me tell you about the robbery." She poured him a cup of tea and handed it to him.

He accepted it and sipped the bitter liquid. He loathed tea, but would drink it if necessary.

"I was on my way to San Francisco to see my nephew—or was it my niece?" She shook her head. "My brains are a little scrambled, I'm afraid. Too much high livin' while I was a youngster. Now, where was I?" She paused. "Yes. I was on my way to San Francisco. This was about two weeks ago, I'd say. It happened about fifteen minutes after we left Pardo. We started to climb the mountains and I was sitting there knitting a new sweater when suddenly the door burst open. That was enough to make me look up from my close work," she said, smiling. "I looked up and saw these two men demanding our money and jewelry!" She sniffed. "I never thought that would happen to me on a train."

"Go on," Spur gently urged.

"Well, naturally I handed over my purse. He didn't think that was enough, and waved his shooter at my neck. I couldn't for the life of me figure what he was doing, and then he said he wanted my pin—my mother's pin that I only wear for special days. It's just an old cameo given to her by one of her suitors years back—worth almost nothing, but he demanded it anyway. I gave it to him. Pretty soon the men left. Well, the train stopped and there was this awful jerk that nearly made me sick in the neck. After about an hour of waiting and inane questions from the train detectives, we started moving again."

"What did these two men look like?" Spur asked.

"The detectives? Well, they were—"

"No," Spur said. "The men who robbed the train."

"Oh!" she said, laughing. Her cheeks reddened and she slapped her knee. "That's good! That's choice!"

Spur smiled. She was enjoying herself.

Agatha Taylor stopped chuckling abruptly, then looked around puzzled. "What was I talking about?"

"The train robbers," Spur said. "You were going to describe them to me."

"Of course. The thinker's not what it used to be. Maybe that sudden jerk on the train knocked it around a little too much. Anyway, one of them was short, fat, with black hair. The other was taller, though he must have been not much more than a youngster, about my nephew Drew's age—or is that Douglas?"

"How old?" Spur asked smoothly.

"About eighteen, maybe nineteen. Blonde hair poked out from under his hat—I remember that part, because it was the yellowest hair I've ever seen in my whole and entire."

"Anything else?" Spur sipped the bitter tea.

"Not so far as I can think. Of course, they wore masks, so I really couldn't see their faces. But one of them might of—yes, he had an ugly scar on his arm, near his hand, that had obviously been stitched up poorly. It was a long scar."

"Was this the kid or the older man?"

She tapped her nose with the end of her fingers, then shook he head. "Can't remember right now. Too much thinking. Come back later, and I'll probably remember more." She lifted the cup to her lips and sipped.

"Thank you, Mrs. Taylor," Spur said, setting his cup down on the table.

"You're not leaving so soon, are you, Mr. McCoy? Can't we sit and talk a while longer? There's not too many folks around here who can sit and talk like we're doing."

"Mrs. Taylor, this may not be any of my business, but why'd you move to Dolmen?"

She smiled. "I don't like crowds."

"Suzanna!" the voice called from below the tree, a woman's voice.

She pressed her back against its truck, balancing her feet on the limb, and tried to look over it to the ground. She couldn't see. Was this a trap, something Lloyd had dreamed up to torment her with?

"Suzanna! Where are you?"

This time she heard the voice clearly—it was Phoebe.

"I'm up here!" she called. "In this tree!"

"Why on earth—never mind. Climb down here. You'll be late for supper."

"Where's Lloyd? Is he with you?"

"No. I'm alone. Come on down!"

She slipped her legs over the branch and carefully, slowly moved down the massive trunk. As her feet touched the ground she turned and saw Phoebe standing before her.

"Phoebe!" she said, rushing to her. Her younger sister took Suzanna in her arms and held her.

"What were you doing up in the tree, Suze? Was a mountain lion after you or something?"

"No. Worse. It was Lloyd."

The two women started back for the mine. "I

don't know what you're talking about."

"He's—he's—oh, I *hate* him!"

"You can't say that. You can't think that. Not until he gives us our money. Lord knows we've earned it."

"Damn him!" Suzanna said, breaking from her sister's arm. "Why did I ever trust a man again? Why?"

"Come on, Suze. Supper's getting overcooked, and I'm getting cold!"

Suzanna reluctantly walked back to the mine. Lloyd wasn't in sight so she went inside and decided to stay there until nightfall.

"Suzanna!" Phoebe called. "Come on. Supper's ready!"

After a few minutes the smell of the simmering food became too much for her. Suzanna was ravenously hungry. She stood and walked out to the fire, where Phoebe was busy dishing out more of the endless pot of stew.

Lloyd squatted on a log thirty feet from the fire, his back turned, eating. Robinson and Willis sat next to each other, as usual. Suzanna accepted the plate of food and a porcelain cup of strong, hot coffee, then returned to the mine, breaking her self-imposed rule —no eating inside.

"You know the best thing about women?" Robinson said from outside.

"No. What?" Willis responded.

"Neither do I!"

The man laughed at the weak joke until Suzanna slammed the plate against the rocky wall.

While walking back to the train, Spur checked his

pocket watch—he had fifteen minutes before it left Dolmen. Maybe another visit to Agatha Taylor would be revealing.

He walked down Oak Street and knocked again.

"Who's there?" the woman said in the same cautious manner, not even opening the door this time.

"Spur McCoy. I was just here."

"Prove it," came the prompt reply. "How do I know you're not some wild Indian?"

"Not many Indians speak English." Still as careful as ever, Spur thought.

After a moment the door cracked open. Mrs. Taylor peered out from behind it and beamed when she saw Spur's face. "Mr. McCoy, it is yourself! Come on in. I've still got some tea."

"I can't stay long," Spur said. "I have to get back to the train before it leaves."

Her face fell. "I see. Oh well, never mind. You're here about the robbery again?"

"Yes. I wondered if you remembered any more details about it—the men who did it, the things that happened—anything."

The corners of her mouth rose half consciously. "Yes. Would you like me to tell you?"

"I would appreciate it."

They moved into the parlor where Spur stood as she rocked and talked.

"Well, we were sitting on the train and I remember mentioning to the woman next to me—no, it was a man. That's right. I remember mentioning to him—no, I've got it backwards. He mentioned to me that one of the fellows—the train robbers—had on a strange kind of boot. Lord knows, I hadn't looked at their boots, but he pointed out the window and by leaning across his lap—he really was a nice man—I could see what he meant. It was on the ground outside in the dirt, clear as all get out, and was one of the darndest things I've ever seen." She stopped suddenly.

"And?" Spur said. "What did it look like?"

"Well, it was the darndest thing. Shaped just like an ace, it was—like the ace of spades. It was the boot's heel. Did you ever see such a thing in your whole and entire?" She looked at him expectantly.

"Can't say that I have."

"Well, this man next to me had. He called it a gambler's heel, because some gambler fellow somewhere had a boot specially made with an ace of spades, since it's the bad luck card and all. He figured that if he carried one around it would only reverse his luck, which had been something awfully fierce. And it worked—the man grew rich. He couldn't seem to lose.

"Then one day he was shot cold dead in the street —he'd just won a whole sackful of money and was on the way to the bank—or was he on his way home?" She shook her head and frowned. "Anyway, the thief not only took his money—he also stole the boot! The man next to me on the train said that it's been making its way around here for ten years or so, but there's probably a few other gamblers that's had boots made with ace heels."

"An ace?" Spur asked.

"That's right—just like in a deck of cards. It was the heel, don't you know—like an upside down heart with a stem sticking down from it. Couldn't miss it if I ever saw it again. The prints showed clear and bright

—that's why the man next to me—what was his name?—saw them and pointed them out to me."

"Thank you, Mrs. Taylor." Spur moved to the door.

"Will you be back?" Her voice shook.

"I'll try. You've been a great help to the Union Pacific, Mrs. Taylor. Thank you."

"You're welcome." She beamed. "Come by any time, Mr. McCoy."

"I will." He waved and left the house.

Spur made it back to the train just as it was preparing to leave Dolmen. He nearly bumped into James Mitchum, who hurried away without speaking as he entered the second passenger car. McCoy went to his seat and leaned back against the cushions, ready to rest for an hour or so until he arrived in Pardo.

While he slept Spur dreamt of aces and grand-mothers and tempting she-dragons who spat words with fire.

CHAPTER SIX

Damn the Union Pacific. The words rolled around James Mitchum's head as he walked into the caboose, sat on the bed, propped up his feet near the oil stove, and took out a box of cheroots. He stuck one of the brown, thin tubes into his mouth and fired it up, then sat puffing, shaking gently back and forth with the train's steady movement.

The goddamned sons of bitches don't trust me anymore! I can find those bastard robbers! Mitchum thought as his face reddened with rage. But the Union Pacific didn't think he could, so they had hired on some damn fool government man who probably didn't know a caboose from a papoose.

He ran a hand through his prematurely gray hair, the frown deepening. They didn't think he could do it. They thought he was scared.

He pulled at the ends of his sparse white moustache, momentarily straightening them from curling around his thin lips. Mitchum knew he was the best detective the Union Pacific had ever hired on, despite the fact that he'd never solved or even witnessed a rail robbery. He'd helped a few old women find their purses, and had caught a pickpocket working the club car, but Mitchum knew he could hold up under direct attack.

Of course, he'd never fought in the war. On his first day in uniform, after being hastily drafted into the army, his whole company had fallen sick from bad meat. By the time he'd been released from the Maryland hospital the war was over.

Mitchum inhaled the smoke and snorted it out through his nostrils. He'd never forgive the army for fucking up his chance of making a career in uniform during the war.

He stood suddenly, glancing at his pocket watch's cracked face: one minute until noon—until this new government detective said he'd meet him in the caboose. Christ; he wished he could dodge this showdown.

The caboose door swung open and a tall, ruggedly handsome man stepped in, towering a half foot over Mitchum. The detective looked up at the man, overwhelmed by his sheer physical size.

"Mr. Mitchum?"

"Yes," he said. "You must be McCoy, the man from the government."

"That I am."

"I got your message and came right away." Mitchum pulled in another drag from the cheroot.

"I figured we should talk," McCoy said, his fists resting on his hip bones.

"I guess we should. After all, we're working—"

"Have you seen them?"

Mitchum seemed startled. "Who?"

"The men who've been robbing the Union Pacific."

"No."

"Didn't think so. Do you have any descriptions of the men, any ideas where they might be holed up?"

"No. I thought that's why they hired the fancy Secret Service man." He scowled. "Look, McCoy, let's get one thing understood right now. I don't like you. I don't want you here. You'll just get in my way."

"More likely the other way around," McCoy said evenly. "After all, I've got authority over you. You're working under my direction."

Mitchum drew in a breath audibly. "I'm *what?*"

"We can work together," Spur said, smiling. "I'm sure you're willing to cooperate with the United States government."

"I—I g-g-guess," Mitchum sat on his bed again, leaning his forearms on his knees.

"Good. I'm going to the dining car. You coming?"

Mitchum looked up blankly, then shook his head.

"It's been a hoot in hell," Spur said, and swung on his heel and exited.

Mitchum shook, his neck muscles tightening, bulging from beneath his pale skin.

"D-d-damn," he stuttered.

Spur McCoy ate a tasty meal of roast beef, stewed tomatoes, corn and coffee, downed a fat wedge of apple pie, then returned to the caboose. A quick check told him Mitchum wasn't there.

He walked through two of the three passenger cars before he found Mitchum sitting beside an elderly woman.

"Mr. Mitchum?" Spur said.

"What?" The voice was instantly hostile. Mitchum turned and glared at him.

"Can we talk for a minute?"

"Sure." The man mumbled some explanation to the woman and stood, then walked with Spur to the rear of the car. "What the hell is it?"

"Calm down, Mitchum. All I want is a map of the area. I can't seem to find one—sure, the engineer's got one, but I'm not climbing up there."

"I—I don't have one."

"Could you draw me one?"

"Of course," he said, sighing.

Moments later, back in the caboose, James Mitchum drew a map. His pen strokes were wide, sweeping, and Spur quickly grew familiar with the territory. The map showed landmarks and towns and abandoned settlements.

"Any other towns that have died, or old forts, or any other places where the robbers might hide?"

After a minute of thought, Mitchum added a few cross marks and letters beside them. Spur took the paper as he handed to him and studied it intently.

"Thanks," he said, and walked out the door. Mitchum might be a little green, but he drew damn good maps, Spur thought.

He sat in the club car, sipping a whiskey as he looked over the map. The towns were strung out like pearls on either side of the tracks: Cheyenne, Laramie City, Rock Springs, Bryan, Pardo, Dolmen—as well as a few others. Small crosses near the town of Pardo drew Spur's attention. Mitchum's careful scrawl read "old mine."

Pardo. Agatha Taylor said the train was robbed

shortly after it left Pardo. The shopkeeper in Green River mentioned that the suspicious man said he usually bought his supplies in Pardo.

Slim leads, Spur admitted, but there could be a connection. McCoy decided to make a careful check of Pardo and the surrounding area—including the mine that Robert Mitchum had so carefully pointed out on his map.

"Mr. McCoy?" a softly feminine voice said.

Spur glanced up and saw Helena Fredrickson standing before him, bending over slightly, the angle enhancing the swell of her breasts.

"Yes, Miss Fredrickson?" Spur rose, lifting the map.

"What's that?" She extended a finger to his hand.

"A map of the Wyoming territory. I had Mitchum draw it up for me." His eyes narrowed. "Why?"

Helena Fredrickson straightened and folded her hands before her. "As security coordinator I should be informed of all events which affect the safety of this train, its passengers and cargo."

"Really?" Spur was unimpressed. "First off, this map isn't an *event*. Second, I understand that you're not working yet—after all, the gold won't be passing through here until the 20th. You've got nothing to protect."

"That's where you're wrong, Mr. McCoy. I have the lives of the passengers to protect, and the United States mail. With all the trouble we've had with thieves," she said, "there's always reason for security."

"I don't think Mitchum's drawing a map for me is your concern." Spur was tired of the woman; of her vain attempts to pretend to be working for her father's train company.

"It's not the map," she said impatiently. "It's what you might find out from it. What are those marks there?" She bent and looked at the map, still gripped in Spur's fist. "There aren't any towns out in those places."

Spur laughed softly, folded the paper and stuffed it down the front of his pants. "If you want it, go ahead and get it."

She blushed and looked away for a moment. "Mr. McCoy! I am a lady, and I won't be subjected to that kind of look!"

"What kind of—*look, Miss* Fredrickson? It's obvious you're trying to do a job, but this isn't the way to do it. If you're bound and determined to make a fool of yourself, go ahead—but leave me out of it."

"I just want to find the robbers!" she said.

Spur shook his head. "You just want to look good in your father's eyes. He's humoring you. You know that. Do you actually think you're going to be any help to me?"

Helena nearly started to dissolve into tears, then straightened her back, pushed out her chest, and set her jaw.

"Obviously not, Mr. McCoy, if you refuse to let me."

He touched her shoulder. "If you want to help, stay out of trouble and try not to disturb me while I'm working."

Helena shook off his touch, stamped her foot and briskly walked away.

Spur one, Helena Fredrickson zero, he thought. As he sat the bench was still warm.

CHAPTER SEVEN

Steve Robinson's stubble-covered, grimy face was transfixed as he pounded into the woman, their groins crashing against each other then parting, only to be drawn almost hypnotically back together.

The woman—perhaps eighteen—squirmed, blew out her breath slowly, and rolled her eyes while staring at the ceiling. The man's administrations, world shattering though they were to him, left her cold.

Robinson, hovering above her on his palms and the tips of his toes, looked down and saw her boredom.

"Goddamn, stupid bitch!" he growled. "Doesn't that feel good?"

"Yeah. Sure." She seemed to be half asleep.

"Shit!" Robinson stroked twice as hard into her, dropped his body onto hers and pinched her nipples savagely.

"Ow!" she complained. "That hurts!"

"You're damn right it hurts," Robinson said. "A

good fuck always hurts. I want you to remember me in the morning—not only deep in your cunt but also right here." He scraped his jagged fingernails over her nipples.

The woman tensed with pain for an instant, then relaxed. "Yes. Hurt me. Hurt me!" Her hips jerked erratically as Robinson continued to pump into her. She grabbed his flexing butt, turned her palms outward and scratched up his back.

"Fuckin' bitch!" Robinson said, squirming under the pain from her nails. "God. Shit!"

"Fuck me. Fuck me raw!" She threw her legs up while simultaneously tightening up around his steel-hard penis.

Shit!" Robinson slipped out of her and drove back forward, sliding along her belly. He reached down to reinsert himself and felt his balls ride up tight and high against his body.

"God. I'm coming!" Robinson yelled as he thrust into the air against her, gushing her sperm out in two foot arcs, to splash down on the woman's breasts.

Below him, she jammed three fingers between her legs and rubbed herself to a frenzy while he lay panting on top of her.

Robinson frowned as he recovered. She's a professional, he thought, and hadn't started acting until the second half of the performance. Even Phoebe Buckland was a better fuck. Still, she was different. He got tired of the same old hole—or holes —day after day.

Robinson stood, hoisted his pants and buckled himself into them. He pushed the black hat firmly onto his head, threw a dollar onto the marble topped dresser, and left without saying a word.

He had work to do.

Steve Robinson was short, slightly overweight, smelly, greasy, and his own man. He knew he was the best and wasn't one to hesitate saying so. By the time little Stevie had turned twelve most of his body had been covered with a fine sheen of hair, which had later grown into the black, curly thicket which drove women wild.

Young Steve's father had told him that was because he was more man than some. Hell, Robinson wondered sometimes if it didn't also make him bulletproof. In his two years of knocking around the west, after countless bank and train robberies and simple holdups, he'd never been shot.

Of course not, he thought, smiling. He was the best and bulletproof to boot. Robinson moved his absurd little body down the street from the saloon to the Western Union office. It wasn't more than a suggestion of a place, a small front room in the only hotel in town, the Bucher.

"Any telegrams for E. I. Edwards?" Robinson asked the timid man behind the counter.

"Yes. I recognize the name. Came in about an hour ago." The thin, bookish man searched his cubbyholes until he found the correct envelope. He slipped it through the bars that separated him from his customers.

Robinson turned and walked out of the hotel to the livery stable. Lloyd had said that they needed another horse; at least, they *might* need another horse if the upcoming shipment would actually pass through this way. Lloyd hadn't talked much about their next job, no matter how much Robinson had threatened to cut off his balls if he didn't.

The thought of Lloyd made him hawk up mucous and spit. The guy was okay, and had some damn good sources of information, but Lloyd just wasn't a born leader. If he'd been running it, things would be different, although he couldn't decide quite how.

Still, he was content to stand beside Lloyd, use him for as long as he possibly could, then either kill him or simply move on. During these past six months with Lloyd, Robinson had made more money than ever before.

Robinson hesitated, looking down at the telegram. Should he open it and read it? No, he thought. The message would be in code, so he couldn't understand it anyway. Besides, Lloyd would kick him if the envelope was opened.

Robinson folded the wire and slipped it into his hip pocket, then went to find the livery stable.

"How about warming me up?" Ray Lloyd asked, staring at Suzanna as they sat near the fire at noon, rubbing their hands.

"Leave me alone, Ray! And keep your hands off me. I don't want to feel your skin next to mine."

"Why not?"

"Why not? After what you did to me? Grabbing me, chasing me through the woods? You're lucky I came back here at all."

"Shit, I was just playing with you. You know that."

"You know you *weren't!*"

"Hell, why am I lucky you came back? What good are you to me? You won't spread your legs; you can't cook, can't do anything."

"Except watch the horses," Suzanna said bitterly.

72

"That's right." His eyes narrowed. "But that's an important part of each robbery. If we come back there and those horses aren't there, we're out of luck." His face softened. "You know, Suzanna, you're quite a looker."

"So are you," she said, then grimaced. She hadn't meant to play his games.

Lloyd raised his eyebrows. "Really?"

"Never mind." Color rushed to her cheeks.

"You like the way I look?" Lloyd pushed out his chest.

Suzanna shrugged. "Maybe not the way you smell, but the way you look. Yes." She stared at the fire. "Damn you!"

Lloyd's mouth dropped slightly.

"Oh hell; you know that! Why do you think I left the train and came with you in the first place? It wasn't the money—which, by the way, you *still* haven't given me. It was you—the way you looked. I don't know." She rested her forehead against a hand propped up on her knee.

Lloyd grinned. "If you feel that way, let's fuck." His voice was low, earthy. He leaned toward her and snaked out his tongue, then thrust it into her ear.

"Stop that," Suzanna said, then pressed against him. "Oh, stop that!"

Lloyd nibbled on her ear.

"God. Oh God!" Suzanna's hands gripped his strong thighs as he worked over her ear. She moved her hands up and pressed against the hardness of his crotch. "Damn you, Ray Lloyd!" she hissed as his mouth moved to hers, and any further unformed words were lost in a clashing of tongues.

* * *

Spur McCoy walked off the train into Pardo, Wyoming territory, a brand new town with six streets and fifty structures. He went to the town's hotel, then the restaurant, the general store, and two saloons, coming up empty each time. The sun broke from the clouds and Spur was quickly aware of how much time he'd spent there fruitlessly. No one seemed to recognize the two men whom Agatha Taylor had described.

Standing at the edge of the broad street covered with two inches of dust kicked up by horses and carriages, Spur pulled out his pocket watch to check the time. As he did the chain broke. He fumbled with it and the watch plummeted to the dust.

Spur bent to retrieve it. As his fingers clasped around it his attention was riveted onto a clear, clean impression in the dirt: it was the sole of a boot, below which was the powerful heel image of an ace.

"Gambler's heel," Agatha Taylor had called it.

Spur retrieved the watch and stuffed it into his pocket. The tracks stretched out with the toes pointed west. He had little trouble following them. Though he lost the trail a few times where a carriage or wagon had driven through, he always found the tracks again. Finally they veered off the street into the livery stable.

He hurried into the place and yelled.

"Hey. Anyone here?"

"Hold your goddamned horses!" a voice said from somewhere behind the building. "I'm taking a piss!"

Spur studied the tracks while he waited; they definitely led into the livery. If Agatha Taylor was right and there were few of these types of boots

74

around, and one of the train robbers had worn one during the last hold up, he may be a step closer to finding the robbers.

"What the hell do you want? Can't a man even piss without somebody bothering him?" The man was thin, balding, angry and sweating profusely.

"I'm in a hurry."

"Yeah? The whole damn world's in a hurry."

"Did a short, black haired, pudgy man come in here today? Maybe an hour ago?"

"Only two men came in today. One, Hotchkiss, came to get his horse re-shoed. The other—I didn't recognize him. He's not from around here."

"Dark haired?"

"Could be. Yeah, come to think of it." He eyed Spur suspiciously. "Why? What do you care? Are you a bounty hunter on the trail of a fast thousand?"

Spur laughed. "Guess again."

"Did I pass up a bundle of money? Is he wanted dead, or alive?"

"What did the man want with you?"

The wrangler shrugged. "Bought a horse—paid cash for it. The finest, strongest, hardest-working horse I had."

"What did this horse look like?"

"Like a horse. Brown, with a white mane and tail."

"Reddish brown or light brown?"

"Reddish brown, a sorrel. Why? What's it to you? Who the hell are you?"

"Did this guy say where he was going?"

"No," the man said, scowling. "Didn't talk much. You a U.S. Marshal or something?"

"Right. I could use your help. I need to find this

75

man. You sure he didn't say where he was going?"

The man shook his head. "No. He wasn't the kind who talked much, and I wasn't damn foolish enough to ask him. He was bad. I could see it in his eyes."

"Did you see which way he left town?"

"North, up into the hills."

"Thanks." Spur left.

Covering the ground in a thirty-foot radius from the stables, he could find no footprints with the distinctive ace heel. The man who'd bought the horse was probably the one who wore the boot.

He pulled the map from his pocket and studied it. The crossed lines that marked the abandoned mine seemed to be four or five miles from Pardo, almost due north. That fit. He turned and walked back to the livery.

"I need a horse," Spur said as the man approached him.

"Okay, lawman. Anything you want, you've got."

An hour later Spur rode the black and white stallion through the trembling aspen and yellow-pine covered foothills, searching for the mine. His only landmark from the map was a craggy mountain top that resembled an owl's head from a certain angle.

Spur rode for two hours, studying the surrounding brilliant green mountains and hills, some capped with snow masses that seemed to have been poured onto them.

Spur was ready to give up when he suddenly turned his back and saw the *owl*. The old mine should be to the left of it, somewhere within sight of the mountain.

He searched, walking his horse quietly through

the area, to hide his approach and to thoroughly cover the ground. He figured the gang—if they were using the mine as a temporary hideout—wouldn't have chosen it if it were readily visible.

Spur sighed and halted the stallion, rubbing its neck. As he looked around he heard the sound of a river splashing down a ravine. He remembered the stream Mitchum had marked on the map.

As Spur listened to the water he heard the unmistakable sound of a woman's laughter.

Robinson rode up to the temporary, tree-crowded corral and tied up the two horses, then dashed through the woods to the mine.

"Lloyd!" he said, darted toward the man who was stiffly poised, Winchester in hand.

"Christ, Robinson!" Lloyd dropped his aim. "Don't worry me like that!"

Robinson shrugged. "Shit, I didn't think—"

"Yeah. You didn't." Lloyd shook his head. "Where's the wire? Did it come?"

"Yeah." He dug it out of his back pocket and handed it to Lloyd.

The man tore open the envelope and studied the message for a moment, then smiled and held it out to Robinson.

"Go ahead. Read it."

Pleased at this show of confidence and trust, Robinson looked at the wire:

"E. I. Edwards, Pardo, Wyoming Territory. Will be arriving 20th with 200 head. Watch for me. I'll be back with the two birds. W. Jones."

"You know what it means?" Lloyd's voice was smug.

"No."

"Didn't think so. This is a note from a friend in New York. $200,000 is being shipped west and it's going through here on the 20th. It's in double eagles."

"Two hundred thousand dollars!" Robinson repeated, then whistled. "Christ, what a job!"

"Yeah. That's why we're going to do it with no mistakes."

Robinson smiled and slammed his fist into his left palm. "That's fuckin' fantastic!"

"The twentieth—that's amost a week sooner than I'd thought. Doesn't give us much time to get ready."

"We can do it," Robinson said defensively.

"I know that. I'm just not sure about Willis."

"Leave the kid alone," Robinson warned. "I'm training him real good. He's picking it up fast."

"He's a pretty good shot," Lloyd said, "but there's room for improvement."

Robinson nodded. "He'll get better." He handed the wire back to Lloyd. "I don't know how you can read those things—those codes. I sure hope it says what you think it does."

"Trust me," Lloyd said. "Just think—in a few days you'll be $50,000 richer."

Robinson smiled, then glanced sharply at Lloyd. "You're not thinking of breaking us up, are you? I mean, that's a lot of money. A man could live a long time on that."

"Don't know. Maybe we'll split for a few months, or a year or so, then get together again. It's getting dangerous to stay in this area—the Union Pacific's mad as hell and they could find us. Besides, if we pull back and disappear for a while, they might think we've gone out of the business. Then when they don't expect it we'll hit the trains again.''

Robinson looked at Lloyd, then shook his head. ''We break up now, we'll never get back together. We'll just go off and get killed or join some other gang.''

Lloyd smiled. ''Probably. That's life.''

CHAPTER EIGHT

"Come on, Phoebe," Chuck Willis said as they crouched near the edge of the shallow, swift streams on its beach. He tickled her side, then slipped his hand up around her breasts.

"Not now," she said. "I'm busy." Phoebe sluiced plates, coffee cups and pots in the fast moving water, scrubbing them occasionally with a handful of coarse horsetail grass stalks and sand.

"Come on." Willis moved on his toes behind her, then pressed his warm crotch against her back. "I've got something for you!"

Phoebe laughed, finished rinsing off a plate, then set it on the sandy beach. "Chuck, can't you wait a minute?"

"No." He stood. "Goddamn it, Phoebe! Come on. It'll only take a few minutes."

Phoebe sighed and set down the last plate. "I'm done now. What'll only take a few minutes?"

Willis unbuckled his belt and pushed down his

pants and drawers. His erection swung up, arching away from his body.

"Chuck!" Phoebe said. "How can I turn down an offer like that?" She opened her mouth and leaned forward on her knees before him.

Willis, his face suffused with excitement and tension, took two steps and touched his penis to her lips.

"Taste me," he said. "Lick the head. Yeah! Jeezus!" Chuck said as he slid into her mouth, pushing until his hairy testicles rested on her soft chin. Phoebe didn't gag as he withdrew and plowed home again. Hot bitch, he thought, pumping down her throat. He felt the wind rush against his half naked body while enjoying Phoebe's incredible tightness and heat. Just as he started to lose control a soft crunching noise to his right shocked him back to reality. He pulled out from Phoebe's mouth.

"Why'd you do that?" she asked, pouting, while wiping her lips on her dress sleeve.

"Someone's coming," Willis whispered.

Phoebe laughed. "I thought *you* were just about to." She licked his throbbing penis.

"I'm serious!"

"It's probably just Steve watching." She took one of his balls into her mouth and sucked hard.

"I heard—ahh. Aahhh."

Phoebe moved up and enmouthed him again. Chuck stood enjoying it and held her head, then pumped into her. He felt his knees weaken as he increased the speed. His mind shifted, the brilliant hues of green and blue around him melting into throbbing blackness as he orgasmed. Chuck's knees buckled and he gripped Phoebe's head for support while very nerve in his body screamed for relief. His hips jerked twice more before Phoebe pulled away for him.

"Mmmm!" she said, licking her lips.

A soft but unmistakable crunch of dead leaves near them forced Chuck Willis' overloaded brain into functioning. With shaking hands he reached down for his pants, but stopped halfway.

Phoebe smiled up at him. "That was wonderful, Chuck. I—"

"Someone's out there," he whispered, laying a hand over her mouth.

She wrapped her fingers around his softening penis. "I told you, it's just Steve."

"Let me go!" He pulled on his clothing and motioned for Phoebe to rise. As she did so they heard another soft crackle in the woods.

Somewhere.

The woman's laughter rang out again across the mountainous area. Spur tied up his horse in a well concealed hollow and moved carefully through the dense undergrowth and mounds of dead leaves. The woman's voice seemed to be coming from near the river.

He quickly found the broad stream, then ducked down behind a tree. Not more than ten yards from him, along the stream's bank, an attractive young woman busily sucked a yellow haired young man's erection.

Spur smiled at the unexpected show, then grimaced. The kid had yellow hair, bright blond, and seemed to match the general description of one of the two men in the holdup. Could he be this lucky, to stumble onto one of the thieves?

But alone in the woods with a woman? Didn't seem likely. He walked slowly back into the trees, circled around and then approached the couple from the other side, where he had more cover. Spur saw the ecstasy on the man's face. He's close, McCoy thought. Might as well let him finish.

A minute later the man's knees buckled and his face twisted in pleasure/pain. Spur walked toward the pair, dashing the final couple of feet as the man looked up and the girl rose. He cleared the last trees and stood on the narrow beach, his Colt in hand.

The woman, a stunning redhead with rings of curls surrounding her head, seemed shocked at Spur's sudden appearance.

"Who are you?" she asked in a slight southern accent.

"I'm unarmed," the man said almost simultaneously. He lifted his hands. "Don't shoot. We don't have no money."

"That's not what I'm after," Spur said. "What're you doing out here? Not the most private place for love making."

The redhead blushed.

"We're not doing nothing," the youth said. "I'm just getting my rocks off. We're camping nearby for the night," he said.

"Bullshit! There's no trails through these hills, and the railroad's five miles to the south." Was this one of the bank robbers? Just because the man was young and blond didn't make him a criminal.

"Railroad?" The redhead looked at Spur, then back to her companion.

"What do you know about the railroad?" Spur asked. The woman was acting suspiciously. She wasn't as good at it as the boy. If they were involved in the holdups, Spur knew they wouldn't be alone, so he kept his voice down.

"Nothing!" the boy said. "We can't pay to ride the train, so we're riding through these parts. I'm thinking about homesteading here."

Spur snorted. "Right. And she's Lily Langtry." Spur stepped closer to the man and aimed for his heart. "If you lie to me, boy, you're going to feel what it's like to die. Soon."

The younger man swallowed hard.

"Are you part of the gang that robbed the Union Pacific?"

The woman started. Spur saw sweat squeeze out on the boy's forehead, unshaded by a hat.

"Fuck no!" he said, his voice shaking slightly. "We don't know about no robberies. What the hell makes you think that? Do you see sacks of money around here?"

"What could a woman and a man, alone, have to do with train robberies?" The redhead's voice was definitely southern.

"I'm not so sure you *are* alone." Spur might not be able to read them completely, but he knew they were lying. Maybe he could shock them into talking. "Cut the crap, both of you! Start talking, fast, or I'll blow your brains out!"

The two stared at him in surprise, then terror.

"No!" the woman said. "I never did anything! I wasn't even with them!"

"Shut your mouth, Phoebe!" the boy said.

"What are you talking about? You never did what? Who's them?"

"I—I only cooked for them. That's all!"

"Quiet!" The blond boy snarled at her.

"That's enough kid!" Spur slashed the .45 across the boy's forehead, jolting him backward. "Tell me, Phoebe. What meals? For whom? The two of you?"

"No," she said, shaking her head. "There's—"

"Jesus Christ, Phoebe! Shut your dumb mouth!" The boy shook with anger.

"There are more of us," the redhead blurted.

"Damn you!" growled the kid, making a lunge for her.

"Don't move," Spur swung the Colt .45 to cover him.

"And don't *you* move, stranger, or you'll get six rounds in your back!" a loud, female voice boomed from behind him.

James Mitchum sat in the club car, watching the monotonous scenery pass by outside the windows. Endless strings of mountains and valleys rushed past as he finished his second shot of whiskey.

Two hundred thousand dollars in gold! It would soon be on his train. His eyes gleamed at the prospects of that much money. If only he wasn't moral, Mitchum thought for the thousandth time. He'd be rich and living the good life somewhere warm and sunny—instead of riding around in these old, uncomfortable boxes.

Of course, people like Helena Fredrickson had their own private cars, and so get the best of both worlds—comfort and the convenience of travel. He'd heard she had had the car hooked to the train so she wouldn't have to stay with the passengers.

How thoughtful of her father, Mitchum thought, smirking. Helena Fredrickson was a pampered rich bitch playing *security coordinator*, whatever the hell that meant, until she tired of it and went back home to her boy friends and dances.

The bitch never even looked at me for more than a few seconds, Mitchum thought. Only whatever was necessary for their brief conversations. Conversations? Mitchum laughed. Helena usually told him what she thought, berated him, and left. Some talk.

He'd tolerate her presence on the train—it was only for a few days, after all. Mitchum knew he could handle her. He lifted the glass and found it empty. Of course, alcohol helped.

Just as he set the glass down Helena Fredrickson walked by. She looked down at him, stopped and frowned.

"Drinking on the job, Mr. Mitchum?" she asked. "Not in the best interests of the passengers or the Union Pacific. At all times you must be at your peak of alertness, your mind clear and unclouded with alcohol." She shook her head as she looked down at him. "I'm afraid I'll have to report this."

"Hell, go right ahead, Miss Fredrickson! Can't a man relax once in a while without some damned woman jumping all over him?"

Helena smiled. "If you want to relax, do it on your own time in the caboose, where you're supposed to socialize. Don't do it out here where you're causing a scene. This won't look good on my evaluation."

"I don't give a damn about your evaluation," he said. "And you started it anyway," he said sullenly.

"I'm getting damned tired of seeing you every time I turn around. Why don't you just leave me alone?"

Helena's face streaked with color. "Mr. Mitchum! May I remind you that I am an employee of the Union Pacific, at least temporarily. You may expect to see a great deal more of me. Besides, you work for me. I have direct control over you." She paused for effect.

"I'm impressed," Mitchum said. "But that damned McCoy outranks both of us. Hell, I'm not afraid of him, and I'm not afraid of you."

"Don't force me to exercise that control. Drinking while on duty is a violation of company rules."

"Ain't that a pisser!"

A woman two seats away looked at Mitchum, shocked, then turned away.

Helena shook her head and sat opposite him, then lowered her voice. "I will not listen to that kind of language. The passengers are starting to look."

"Hell. Let them look! I don't give a good goddamn!" he said, but his voice was considerably softer.

"Mr. Mitchum, please!"

He nodded. "All right, Miss Fredrickson. I'm not drunk—though I wish to Christ I was. I'll strop drinking if you leave me the hell alone."

Helena's lips tightened into an artificial smile. "Of course. But if that's what you want, don't flaunt outrageous behaviour." She rose and walked off without further comment.

Mitchum stared down at his empty whiskey glass.

"Shit," he said, and rose. He walked out of the club car to the caboose, where he collapsed onto the hard, thin bunkbed and stared at the wooden ceiling above him. Maybe he should quit working for the Union Pacific earlier than he'd planned. Perhaps it was time.

James Mitchum had hired on as a detective because he thought the free travel would be a great way to see the country. Now, after seven months of endless scenery changes and the steady sway of the trains behind him, Mitchum couldn't wait to leave and find a real job somewhere else.

Not yet, he told himself. Not until the big gold shipment came through. After that, he'd do something else—anything else. The Union Pacific obviously didn't trust him any more, so he saw no reason for staying.

Mitchum burped and relaxed against the bed, staring up at the overhead, thinking what he'd do with two hundred thousand dollars.

CHAPTER NINE

Helena Fredrickson went to her private car and crossed to her trunks that were pushed up against the wall below the curtained window, knelt and searched through them. Where was that book?

Around her, the car dripped with elegance. Tasselled, stuffed couches and chairs, mirrors and ferns, silver ashtrays, a lushly thick carpet covered the entire floor—and everywhere the glint of gold plate.

At the bottom of the second trunk she found it beneath a pile of petticoats. She took out the leather bound volume greedily and closed the trunk, then sat beside the window, oblivious to the vistas of blue-green hills passing outside. Helena looked at the book's title: *Detective Work Today.*

She frowned, hoping that E. R. Walton knew what he wrote of.

Helena glanced at the first paragraph and read it quickly:

* * *

"So you want to be a railroad detective? Now is the time! The rail companies have crossed the west and are desperate for able ablebodied men to help them run smoothly while braving the perils of the wild, untamed frontier."

Helena frowned at the word *men*. Already the book was annoying her. She hadn't bought it—her father had given it to her before the trip out west, in case she needed help. Though she had vowed not to read it, Helena felt she was losing control of the situation—both McCoy and the detective had gotten the best of her, as much as she was loathe to admit it —and so she was open to any help. She returned her attention to the book.

"Life on the rails is fraught with danger, excitement, and thrills. Indian raiding parties may descend at any time, force the train to a stop, and board to collect scalps from the helpless passengers. Desperate train robbers, who care for nothing but money, regularly strip the passengers and the express cars of all valuables and cargo. At every turn the detective's life is challenged. You'll never be able to sleep or rest while at work. But you'll have the satisfaction of helping your fellow man while enjoying the freedom of the rails as well. Yes, free travel is an important part of your detective work, as well as solving crimes and holding off robbers. You too, dear readers, can be a railroad detective!"

Helena flipped through the book for five minutes, then threw it into the corner.

"Stupid book," she said. It was a useless compendium of hair-raising tales of *true* detective adventures with one chapter concerning detective work, most of which was useless. It didn't contain one shred of knowledge she could put into practice, and must have been written for people who dreamed of becoming detectives but who never would.

E. R. Walton was probably a newspaper writer, and hadn't left his sensational style behind him.

Helena leaned back in the chair, resting her hands on the stuffed red velvet arms, and stared out the window. At least she was actually doing something! She wasn't like most of the people who'd read the book and then went back to tilling the soil or breaking horses.

Honestly, Helena Fredrickson, she told herself, thinking you need a book to help you out of your problems! All you have to do is sit down and think for a while.

Was she disappointed in the job so far? Helena had to nod. It wasn't as glamorous as she had hoped—in fact, it could be downright uncomfortable. She didn't like to be closed up in the cars all day, without the option of going outside.

Then there were the times when the train jolted suddenly, which nearly always scared her to death. And she couldn't quite dispel the fear that the train would leap off its tracks and go plunging down a ravine. After all, it sped along at forty miles per hour!

She shook off the fears. She was here, on the train, and she wasn't going back home to face her father, not after the fuss she'd made. No. Like it or not, she was on the job for good until the gold was safely to Sacramento.

About James Mitchum and Spur McCoy, Helena thought, and sighed. She couldn't figure out the men —they were complete opposites, but alike. Mitchum broke every rule but still maintained his position.

Spur McCoy seemed to make his own rules, but she supposed that's what came from working for a government organization.

She couldn't decide how to handle the men. No matter how she treated them, kind, sweet, or cooly professional, she couldn't get them to do what she said. Both men had walked over her, even laughed at what she was trying to accomplish.

Helena stopped her train of thought. Just what *was* she trying to do? She paused for a moment, then smiled. "I am trying to improve the security of the Union Pacific trains in order to stop the rash of robberies that have occured on them."

She was pleased with the answer, but quickly frowned. That might be the larger goal, but Helena knew that she was simply a bored rich girl looking for adventure, tired of sitting around the house all day watching the servants work.

Helena rose and paced nervously in the car. She was aware of the danger she'd placed herself in, and was quite surprised that her father had ever let her go, but then wondered if he'd asked Spur to watch her as much as the gold.

She sighed and turned toward the club car. It must be serving by now, and she suddenly realized she was ravenous.

"Don't move your cute little butt," the woman said to Spur's back. "What the hell were you two doing to let him surprise you like that?"

"Nothing," the blond haired man said. "We were just—"

"Never mind! I can imagine."

94

Spur kept his eyes on the pair before him. Who was the second woman? He certainly hadn't expected to find two females with the gang.

"All right, pretty boy. Lay your gun down on the ground. Slowly. Don't think I won't shoot your balls off just because I'm a woman."

Spur hesitated. A slug slammed into the ground two inches from his right foot.

"I said lay it down! Now!"

Spur bent and gently laid the Colt on the sand. The two in front of him visibly relaxed.

"Now turn around real slow. I'm getting tired of looking at your butt."

Spur moved cautiously in a half-circle and saw the woman. She was another stunning redhead, with flashing eyes and a wicked smile playing on her face. She was dressed in a leather skirt and red and white striped shirt, hefting a Winchester. She eyed him for a moment, then whistled.

"Oooowhee! God, what a fine figure of a man you are, stranger! You put the men around here to shame!"

"Phoebe started talking," the boy said. "Talking about things she had no business talking about." He moved toward the other woman.

"Suzanna, I only said—"

"That's okay, honey."

"But—" Phoebe's face crumpled into a frown.

"It doesn't matter anymore. Let's get this guy back to the mine and figure out what to do with him."

"Kill him," Willis said. "Right here and now. That's what Robinson or Lloyd would do."

Suzanna hesitated, staring at him. "Seems such a

waste of a good man. Hell, I wouldn't mind seeing him buck naked. It'd be a nice change of scenery, and I bet he's got a big one.''

''I don't get many complaints,'' Spur said.

Suzanna scowled. ''Keep quiet, pretty boy.''

''Quit stalling!'' the blond said. ''You always said you were as tough as any man, as good a shot. Go ahead, Suzanna. Here's your chance to prove it. Shoot the bastard. He knows who we are and probably what we're up to. We can't let him go now.'' He grinned and moved closer to her. ''What's the matter, Suze? Can't do it? Are you afraid? Will you finally admit it?''

''Can I say something?'' Spur asked.

''No!'' Suzanna said. She turned to Phoebe. ''I think we should let Lloyd handle this, don't you? Maybe he'd want to question him.''

The blond grinned. ''You're scared. I knew it. You're acting like every woman acts—you can't do nothing unless a man tells you to.''

''That's not true!'' Phoebe said, sniffling. ''She's not like that, Willis!''

''Maybe I just want to keep him around in case I need a *real* man to warm me up, not a yellow haired boy.''

''You bitch!'' Willis said. ''You're just like Robinson says you are.''

She smiled and turned her head. ''Willis!'' she called.

Spur dove for the Colt, gripped its handle and jumped to his feet. Suzanna, taken by surprise, leveled her rifle at him while Spur lined up on her with his weapon.

''Stupid bitch!'' Willis said.

''Shut up!'' Spur motioned with the short barrel.

"Unless you're going to use that thing, little lady, I suggest you drop it. I don't have any qualms about shooting a woman when she's ready to return the favor. Drop it. Now!" His words cut through the air.

Suzanna stared at him, mixed emotions playing on her face, and she slowly bent to place it on the ground.

"No!" Willis said. "Lloyd! Hey Lloyd!"

"Quiet!" Spur warned, gesturing with the revolver.

Suzanna laid the rifle on the dirt.

"Fine. Now all of you into the water." He pointed to the stream.

"What?" Phoebe said, gripping Suzanna's hand.

"You heard me. Into the water. Move it!" Spur motioned with his Colt again.

The two women and young man reluctantly walked to the bank and waded in to their ankles.

"Deeper," Spur said. "Come on!"

They trembled with the chill of the melted snow water as they walked in to their knees; Suzanna's face seemed enraptured as she shivered and stared at Spur.

"Farther!" he said. When they were in to mid-thigh, clutching each other to keep warm, Spur smiled. "Now all of you, turn around. Face the other bank."

"Why?" Willis asked, his face crimson with embarrassment. "You going to shoot us, one by one? Are you such a coward you can't kill us while we're looking at you?"

"Shut your fuckin' mouth," Spur said. "Turn around and stay there. Don't move, or you're dead."

The two women followed his instructions, with

Willis doing the same a moment later. Once all backs were turned Spur picked up the woman's rifle and dashed into the forest.

Since they were up to their thighs in water it would take them a few more seconds to follow, which should be plenty of time for him to find his horse and get the hell out of the area. He'd be back—but not alone.

Spur dodged a mouldering, fallen pine trunk, jumping over it like a fence, aware of the noise his fast exit was causing but unable to prevent it. Speed was what counted now.

He took his bearings as he ran. His horse should be in a hollow to his right about one hundred yards ahead. McCoy glanced over his shoulder—no signs of the trio following him. Maybe they were still standing up to their butts in ice cold water, he thought, grinning.

He didn't know who the Lloyd character was, and he didn't want to find out—not just yet. Spur sped through the virgin forest, tramping through huge piles of skeletal aspen leaves and browned needles, alarming nesting birds overhead into flight.

Spur stepped over another fallen log and felt his foot sink into a gooey mud eight inches deep. He jerked his leg up and away from it, but the mud wouldn't let him go. Sweating, knowing three or possibly four people were following him, Spur relaxed his foot into the mud, practically knelt to gently move his boot so that it stuck straight down into the goo, then lifted it out with a slow, constant upward pressure.

Seconds later he dashed through the trees, avoiding other mud holes fueled by hidden springs and mucked with centuries of organic matter.

He cleared the last dozen feet and turned to the hollow.

The stallion wasn't there.

Had it been found and taken? Spur glanced around him—he remembered the flat-topped lightning struck pine tree on his way to find the woman's laughter. His horse was still up ahead.

Spur struck out again, his breath wheezing from the effort, and spotted a likely place to his right ten yards away.

Just as he was hitting his speed a dark figure stepped out from the woods ahead of him, rifle out and aiming for his heart.

"Don't move, bastard!" the man said, grinning.

CHAPTER TEN

Spur dove, rolled on his shoulder through the heaps of dead leaves and jumped to his feet behind a thick tree as a gunshot cracked through the air.

"Damn you!" the tall man said.

Spur plowed two slugs into the earth seconds after the man had scrambled for cover. He cautiously peered over the edge of the tree as his assailant peppered the area with hot lead.

A deadly rattle from below the thick ground cover at his feet froze Spur in position. He glanced down, studying the leaves, and saw them undulating gently, as if something long and thin passed underneath.

Though rare, rattlesnakes were sometimes found in the Wyoming foothills. The movement passed within two inches of his legs—then halted abruptly.

"Hey, you still there, asshole?" a voice called.

Spur answered with fire, half his attention directed to the unseen but potentially deadly enemy near his legs. If he moved suddenly the snake could do the gunman's job. Spur didn't like the idea.

On a glance upward he saw the figure moving through the trees. Spur followed him with his gaze, blasting two slugs inches from the man. The rattle at his feet grew in intensity, and he seemed to see the leaves circle, as if something were coiling up beneath them.

"Shit," Spur said. He knew his opponent had moved quite a distance—if he hadn't been distracted by the snake the man would be dead by now. McCoy knew if he didn't move soon the gunman could circle around and approach him from behind. But the snake—

He lifted his right foot slowly, gently, moving as few leaves as possible. As he did the snake seemed to move closer, with some violent jerkings—the rattles, probably. Spur halted his foot momentarily, then continued to raise it.

A wide shot from his right warned Spur he had to move soon. He pulled his foot up another three inches, shifted it over slightly then stamped down on what he hoped was the snake. He savagely rammed his sole against the leaves and dirt—but saw the snake's retreat.

Damn him!

Spur slipped around a tree, waited a second, then set out to follow the man—probably a member of the train robbing gang. Spur passed as quietly as possible through the dense tree growth, following the man's movements as far as he could determine them.

He halted behind another tree. The forest seemed absolutely still around him until he heard the distant rustle of dry-as-bones leaves. Spur slowly followed, saw a foot-long chunk of wood lying on the ground before him, and hefted it. Might not hurt to cover some of his own tracks, so to speak. He lifted the log, swung it back, then threw it thirty feet. It landed with a loud crash which was immediately followed up by several blasts from the other man's weapon.

Spur shifted his position to bring him behind the man—he was several yards further to the east than he'd thought. As Spur moved again he suddenly stopped—he heard rustling behind him.

Someone was stalking him.

Probably one of the three from the river—perhaps the fiery haired woman, Spur guessed, smiling as he remembered her. He ignored the danger to his rear for the moment—he'd deal with that later. First the tall man . . .

Spur kept a small part of his concentration on the tracker behind him as he scanned the area ahead. The man stood still, somewhere. Spur spotted the tree he'd last figured the man would be behind, reloaded, and fired a round into it. No return of fire.

Strange. The rustle behind him, though still faint, grew closer. He'd lost the man in front and now someone closed in behind. Spur was running out of time.

He let his instinct tell him what to do. Forget the dead leaves and his pursuer. He ran at a 45-degree angle across the woods, figuring that the man had changed course again. Spur knew that if they didn't alter their relative positions chances are they'd meet —sometime.

He kicked through centuries of humus, the garbage of nature, while reloading his Colt. Spur dropped one bullet, and counted that as a minor slip considering the terrain. Since he was making so much noise he couldn't hear the motions of the other two. He was running sound-blind.

Spur halted for an instant—and in that second he placed both men. He set off again directly toward the fleeing man, not thinking how close his pursuer actually was.

He could secrete himself behind a tree or in a valley, then ambush the man, but that meant losing the other one. Spur wouldn't take that chance—if these were actually the thieves he didn't suppose he'd get a second chance with them.

Something snapped in his brain like a dry twig, the kind that smokes when you pop it apart. Spur stopped—the man was ten yards ahead. He circled gently, going at strange angles, constantly moving back and forth to cover as much ground as he could to hide his exact position. Had the man moved?

No. Spur saw him at once—black clothing, tall, lean, lanky. McCoy viewed the man in profile. He raised his aim as something heavy and mean dropped down atop him from a branch high overhead.

Spur felt hard bones and fists and boots on him. A hand slammed into his face as his Colt fell from his hand and landed beneath the tree on a bare patch of ground. He deliberately fell backward, crushing the man beneath him with a crunch. Spur pulled the hands from his chest, rammed his elbows into the man's tender armpits and shrugged the heavy body off.

McCoy swung around easy—the man lay panting on the ground, his face bright with rage. Spur moved to retrieve his weapon and stopped when the lean man emerged from the trees.

"We finally get to eyeball each other," he said, and stooped to lift Spur's gun, which he stuffed inside his belt.

Spur fought the urge to kick the downed man savagely and attack the other, knowing he couldn't win. He stood still, tense, frustrated, mad as hell. He'd bide his time.

"I don't suppose you'll give that back to me," he asked.

The thin man laughed. "No. You won't need it where you're going." He turned to look at the other man. "Robinson, you still in one piece?"

Robinson shook his head rapidly, brushed himself off, and rose to his feet. "Yeah, I guess so." He was still dazed.

"Good. Let's get back."

"Not before I kill him," Robinson said, drawing his weapon.

"No."

"Shit, Lloyd! You can't tell me what to do!"

"I can if you're still working for me. Are you?"

"Well, well shit! Guess so."

"Then do as I say."

Robinson looked at the other man, and Spur saw the hatred behind the dark eyes.

"We're not going to kill him here and now." He looked at McCoy, smiling sarcastically. "Let's make it last. After all, this man nearly cost us $200,000. I want him to know what I think of him."

"Okay," Robinson grumbled.

He walked to Robinson and took a rope from his belt. "Turn around," he said, approaching Spur.

He did so and felt the bite of the rope cutting off the circulation in his wrists. His blood pounded hard against the ropes but couldn't pass them.

"What should we do with him?" Robinson asked.

"Keep him in the mine for now. Let him worry

how he's gonna die."

Robinson grinned.

Spur felt the other man yank at the ropes, then was pushed back through the forest. He wrestled with the knots around his wrists but they held. Mad as hell at having been tricked, Spur walked sullenly along with the two men, waiting for an opportune moment.

Then minutes later Spur sat fifty feet inside the entrance to the mine. It was as far as light penetrated. His muscles screamed for relief from the ropes. With his arms tied behind him and his ankles before him Spur couldn't find a comfortable position in which to sit. He stretched his feet out and studied the knots around his ankles.

It shouldn't be too difficult to free his legs—if he could use his hands. Spur's attention was diverted from the knots when he heard someone approaching. The woman he'd heard called Phoebe walked up to him, carrying a flimsy white garment.

"Hello," he said.

She looked guardedly at him. "I—I'm glad they didn't kill you."

"So am I."

"I mean," she said, biting her lip, "I don't like to see people getting hurt." She laid the chemise down on the mine floor.

"And you stay with men like those?" Spur shook his head. "Maybe you don't know what you want."

She shrugged and started unbuttoning her dress. "Oh. Would you turn your head, mister? I have to change—I'm doing the clothes washing this afternoon."

"Would you be mad if I didn't?"

Phoebe smiled. "No. In fact, I'd be insulted if you

did!" She quickly loosened the buttons down the back, wiggled from the bodice and sleeves, and let the dress slip off to the ground. She stood before Spur fully naked as the soft light filtering into the mine from the distant entrance turned her skin to flawless marble.

Spur felt an erection painfully poke between his legs as he looked at Phoebe's full breasts and the flaming red patch of pubic hair. He looked up at her face and she laughed.

"Like what you see, mister?" She stood relaxed, her weight on one foot, as she brought a hand to her breast. "I like to touch myself. Sometimes when I'm alone, or sometimes when a man's around." She stared into his eyes. "I like it when a man watches." Phoebe rubbed her right nipple between her thumb and forefinger, then switched to the other. They stood up hard and firm. Phoebe gasped and slid both hands between her legs, where she fingered the red hair and then moved into it, parting her lips. "What do you think?" she asked, breathy.

"I like it. Don't stop." Spur's penis strained against his pants, making an obvious bulge.

Phoebe's eyes grew wide as she saw his erection. "I guess you're not lying. I wonder what you'd think if I did this?" She turned around, bent over and spread her lips.

Spur looked up into her mystery. "Damn, Phoebe! You're one hot woman! The way you're touching yourself, you're making me crazy! If you'll just untie my hands I'll shove a finger right up there!"

She turned back around and smiled. "Sorry. I can't do that. If I did, Lloyd would kill me." She thrust a finger inside herself, her face transfixing,

107

eyes closed, chin high, breath puffing out. Phoebe's hips slowly circled as she fingered herself.

"Why use a finger when you can have the real thing?" Spur asked. He shoved his hips up to emphasize the point. Damn the woman for tormenting him! If he couldn't break loose, maybe he could talk her into untying him.

She stopped and removed her finger, then smiled. "Can't. I have the washing to do." She slipped the chemise on and strode out, carrying the dress with her.

"Bitch!" Spur yelled as her laughter diminished and faded.

Spur woke as his chin dropped to his knees, startled that he'd fallen asleep. It was night. Fifty feet in the distance, a tiny fire flickered at the mouth of the mine. Spur saw a figure pass before it; probably one of the men on watch. Everything else looked quiet.

He straightened up slowly and looked around him —with what little light he had Spur could see no one near him. They must sleep near the entrance, he thought, or perhaps around the fire. He tugged at the ropes. No dice. They held.

Spur cursed silently and moved his arms out of the uncomfortable position in which he'd slept and felt something slice into his finger. Spur winced and gently felt behind him—it was a sharp rock, probably split to a near razor's edge by the dynamite blast.

He moved his hands until the rope rubbed against the rock edge. With luck he could cut it. As he worked Spur felt sweat bead on his forehead. Above him a trickle of dust fell from the rock ceiling which was supported by wood timbers. The mine had probably been dug in a hurry, and Spur wasn't completely comfortable inside it.

He scraped the rope against the rock, feeling individual fibers snapping. Spur figured he was halfway through. Just a few minutes more and he'd be free.

An ominous rumble above him made Spur stop.

No. God no, Spur thought. The timbers shook while more dust spilled onto him.

He looked up to see the roof explode into fragments and cascade down. Spur rolled on his shoulder away from the falling dirt into the darkness of the mine as he ears rang with the sound of tons of earth roaring and smashing downward.

CHAPTER ELEVEN

Suzanna paced before the fire, shivering in her three coats and silk underwear. She pretended to dislike standing watch, but didn't really mind. It was only four hours, after all, and she liked the solitude, something she rarely got to enjoy. Pacing to keep warm and remain alert, Suzanna listened to her companions softly breathe and mumble around her. Undisturbed by their thoughts or actions, she could think.

Suzanna was the kind of woman that men said thought too much, and she knew what they meant. She wasn't a giggling young maiden. When she'd reached maturity Suzanna had decided to act her age, no matter what any man thought about it.

She smiled as she glanced at Chuck Willis, his face sideways on his boot pillow, mouth open. A noise behind her startled Suzanna. Something passed through the bushes outside the mine. Probably a small animal, she thought. Maybe a coyote.

Suzanna shivered and sat beside the warmth of

the fire. She pictured the creature in her mind: a vicious set of glistening jaws, stretching wide apart to tear the flesh off her bones in huge chunks, ripping, growling deep in its throat.

Stop it, she told herself. Don't talk yourself into being scared. You know it's only in your mind.

Damn me. I've been so good on watch, she thought. I haven't been frightened for months now. It must be that lawman they'd caught today. If he'd discovered the hideout, someone else could do the same.

Lloyd had mentioned that they'd be moving at dawn and so Suzanna had started packing things. Lloyd had also said that the move wouldn't affect the robbery two days in the future.

A rumble above her jolted Suzanna out of her reverie. She had passed into a light trance, hypnotized by the fire. Coming out of it she looked above her. Everything seemed still. She stood, walked into the mine, and felt it shake.

Suzanna's feet gave way under her, throwing her to the ground. She struck hard, crying out as a rock jabbed her back.

"What the fuck?" Lloyd said, rising from his sleep, his face a mask of confusion.

The others woke as Suzanna struggled to her feet. Three yards from her a solid wall of dirt and rocks poured down. Lloyd, Robinson, Willis and Phoebe rushed from their beds, grabbing boots and weapons, and ran from the mine. Lloyd helped a struggling Suzanna to her feet and hauled her out with him as the mine continued to collapse, sending a huge dust cloud boiling out from the entrance into the sky, where it drifted white against black.

"Anyone hurt?" Lloyd asked as they stood huddled before the mine. "No? Good. Guess we waited one too many days to move."

"We should've left that place a long time ago," Robinson said. "Months ago. I told you that. We all knew it wasn't safe."

"Robinson, shut up! This isn't the time for your stupid remarks," Suzanna said.

Phoebe clung to Willis, who held her tenderly and kissed her hair. Robinson saw them, laughed and brushed the dust off his clothing. When the collapse had halted, they went back to the mine's opening. Though dust had quenched the fire, they used touch and starlight to determine how many of their belongings—if any—remained. They found saddles, ammunition, food—nearly everything, covered with a quarter inch of dust.

Suzanna smiled, then laughed. It wasn't as bad as she'd thought. They wouldn't have to start over again. Then her face darkened.

Phoebe noticed it immediately. "What's wrong?" she asked. "Did you lose something?"

"Yes. Well, no," she stammered. "Hell, I know it's stupid, but that man's still in there."

"Man?" Then Phoebe remembered.

"So what?" Robinson countered. "He'd be dead in the morning anyway. Looks like nature took care of the job for us. There's no way he could have survived that. It must have fallen on top of him."

"Maybe," Lloyd said.

"It did."

"Look, Robinson, I—"

"Hey, Lloyd, where are we sleeping for the rest of the night?" Willis asked.

He looked at the stars. "Only about an hour until morning. We'll stay up and talk over plans."

"And I'll convince you to let me be there with you while you do the next robbery," Suzanna said.

Lloyd jabbed the air before him with a finger. "Drop that subject, Suze. Right now. The last thing I need's your damn nagging."

"I'm cold," Phoebe said, huddling next to Chuck.

"Someone make a fire," Lloyd said.

Robinson fell to it as Suzanna stared up at the sky, watching the stars fade in and out as clouds obscured them momentarily while passing overhead.

"Suze?" Phoebe asked, coming up beside her.

"Hmmm?"

"Do you think Lloyd will ever give us the money?" she asked in a low voice.

"I don't know, Phoebe. I just don't know." She took her sister's hand. "After tonight, all I really want to do is rob a train."

Phoebe gasped. "Really? I thought you were just joking."

"No. Tonight—we could have been instantly smothered without warning if the cave-in happened a little closer." She shook her head. "I'm not going to just sit by and let a man tell me what I can and can't do. I'll do anything, the more dangerous the better, simply because I never know when I'll get the opportunity again." She seized her sister's shoulders. "Do you see what I mean?"

"Yes. Yes, Suzanna, but you're hurting me!"

She froze, released her sister and rubbed the woman's shoulders. "I'm sorry!" she said, and pulled her into a tight embrace.

"If you think he won't give us the money, let's leave today." Phoebe said.

"No. Not until the big robbery. $200,000, Phoebe! I can talk him into letting me help. And then he'll have to give us some of it."

She pushed her sister gently away. "No. I'll ask again at breakfast. If he won't give us the money I'm leaving—I just can't stand it here anymore." She pouted. "Since I'm up, I might as well dust off the dishes and pots. They must be dirty." She walked into the mine.

Suzanna stood in shock. Was this the demure, shy young Phoebe she'd taken away from her stuffy family? Suzanna realized she'd changed too, along with her sister. Whatever else Ray Lloyd had done for them, he'd forced them to grow up.

The mine shook for ten seconds. Spur coughed dust as he lay flat on the ground while the rumble of the last ton of earth echoed through the mine, then died. A few rocks rolled onto him, and he was covered with dirt, but the ceiling above him held. Spur had moved just in time.

In utter darkness Spur wrenched at his wrists. The last fibers in the rope burst apart. After untying his feet he stood, stamping and rubbing his hands to pump blood back to his extremeties. As he did so he looked around. Spur couldn't see the fire, the ceiling, even his hand in front of his face.

He had been sealed in, perhaps permanently?

Spur felt around for the walls, and after two seconds of boldly walking forward his palms contacted a rough, cold surface. He followed the wall until he came to a huge rock and dirt pile. After feeling it for a moment Spur frowned. Even if he had a shovel it'd take him two days to move that much earth. By that time he'd be out of air.

Spur thought about everything he'd ever learned about mines. Air shafts, he remembered. Most mines had air shafts. He had to carefully move deeper into the mine, avoid drop-offs and find an air shaft.

Spur sneezed as he shuffled through the darkness away from the pile, stumbling over rocks that had been freed by the cave-in. He still breathed dust. Spur's feet hit something and he stopped abruptly. He reached down and grabbed it. A rope. He stretched it between his hands and snapped it. Strong, too. Running one hand over it he checked its length. Should be long enough in case he had to climb out. McCoy coiled it and slung it over his shoulder.

He walked on through the gloom, sniffing the air. There had to be an air shaft, he thought as he took another step and stretched out his left foot.

Just after he'd shifted his weight Spur felt his foot pushing against air. He couldn't compensate in time and stumbled, then fell for two terrifying seconds.

Spur landed in a foot of loose dirt, taking the impact on his shoulder. He shook his head and blinked. If it had been dark around him before, it seemed thicker now—almost seething, boiling, increasing in blackness.

He felt around him and discovered he was in a small shaft not more than nine feet across. Spur pushed up on his toes and reached above him— nothing but solid rock walls. He'd fallen at least eight, maybe ten feet. Or more. His body ached but he couldn't detect any broken bones.

Spur felt the rope's absence from his shoulder. A quick search on hands and knees produced the rope, which he hung around his neck. Spur then ran his palms over the rock wall, searching for crevices and cracks which he could use as hand and toe holds.

He found the edge of a fissure that had been picked into the rock during the mine's creation above him, and his boots located an adequate ledge on which to stand two feet from the ground. Spur gripped the protrusion above him and hoisted himself up, resting his boots on the ledge. Feeling around above him, he found two more hand holds, gripped one, hauled himself up, and slid his boots over the wall until they found another place to lodge themselves.

Two minutes later Spur pulled himself out of the shaft. He dusted himself off, took his bearings, and continued walking deeper into the mine. The air had stilled somewhat, and the dust that had rushed down the tunnel like a fireball had nearly settled. Spur smelled the air and searched for the slightest possible mutation in the blackness around him. There had to be an airshaft somewhere.

On impulse he cocked his head back and looked above him. He couldn't see anything, but as he walked with his head thrown back Spur felt cool, fresh air rush across his face.

He immediately halted and stepped back into the flow. Somewhere above, he knew. But where? Spur's hands stretched out and he was surprised that they didn't touch the ceiling—in some parts of the mine the overhead had been within a few inches of his head. Here however, it had apparently raised. Glad I brought the rope, Spur thought, grimacing.

As he stood in total darkness, pondering the problem, a dull purple light appeared above him, then cascaded down into the mine, bathing him in unreal violet hues as he stepped into it.

The color melted into blue, then shifted to orange. Sunrise, Spur realized. The air shaft started three feet above him, and extended upward another fifteen feet. Spur saw a thick pole stretched across its entrance as the light brightened to dazzling day. If he could throw the rope around it he wouldn't have to climb the walls. Probably a good thing, Spur thought, since they seemed smoother above.

He took the rope from his neck and, holding the end in his left hand, threw the coil up. It struck the side of the shaft and fell back noisily. Spur picked it up, coiled it and corrected the angle and power of his throw, and hurled it. The rope sailed around the pole and then lodged against it.

He gently shook the rope's end. For an instant the coil seemed ready to fall free of the pole, but it shifted and plummeted down the opposite side. Spur caught it and pulled the ends. The log seemed strong enough to support his weight.

McCoy gripped the rope in both hands above him, jumped up onto it, and pulled himself up watching the rock walls pass by as he grunted.

After ten grueling seconds Spur made it to the top, strained his shoulder to grasp the wooden frame around the opening, then pushed against the crossbeam. It didn't move. Spur couldn't squeeze past it, and he certainly wasn't going down again.

"Goddamnit!" he said, and plowed the flat of his hand up against it. The pole gave a bit, encouraging another attempt. The third blow knocked the pole free. Spur groaned as he lifted his torso out of the shaft, threw a leg out, and then fully stepped from it, his eyes blinded by the sun shining in a cloud-white sky.

Spur looked around him and saw the owl mountain to his right. He walked down the hill and then back near the mouth of the mine. Spur had lost his gun, but his horse could still be in the woods. If not, the rail tracks were only a three or four mile walk.

Spur's stomach growled—no food in there for a while. Damn it, at least he was still in one piece. He had something to be glad of.

CHAPTER TWELVE

Spur carefully surveyed the mine's entrance from a secluded position, but he saw no movement, no signs of the gang. They'd either been killed in the collapse or had moved in the night.

After waiting a few minutes, Spur walked to the mine and looked it over. They'd taken their belongings and left. Great, Spur thought. They were still alive.

It would have been easy if the mine's collapse had killed them. Too easy.

Spur hiked a half mile back to his horse, which he found standing placidly among the trees where he had tied him. He led the stallion down to the river, let it drink his fill, then set out on a cautious exploration of the area, searching for the gang's new hideout. He checked two other mines, a cave, and even a lean-to, none of which were on Mitchum's map. He found no trace of the five member gang.

After an hour of searching Spur headed back for Pardo, arriving there at 10:20. The next train east wouldn't be in until noon. Spur returned his horse to the livery stable, then walked into the only saloon in town. He ordered a beer and stood drinking it slowly. He could ask around town again, describe the five, maybe pick up some information while he waited.

Steve Robinson and Chuck Willis played cards before the huge fireplace, now alive with flames. Ray Lloyd stared out the window of the old cabin, hands on his waist, wrapped in thought. Phoebe sat mending clothes, and Suzanna drummed her fingers on the rickety table.

"I'm bored," she said flatly.

"Tough shit, Suzanna," Robinson countered.

"We're staying out of sight for a while," Lloyd said, turning away from the window. "No sense in showing ourselves if we don't have to. That government man who found us might have told someone else where we were. We'll stay put for a couple more hours."

"But we have a fire," Suzanna protested. "Anyone can see the smoke coming from the chimney."

"You're not going outside," Lloyd said cooly.

"Fine." She changed the subject. "You know, I can't believe that man's dead."

"Of course not," Robinson said, grinning. "You're lame brained. Hell, he was right under the collapse. That sure was a good idea to put him there, wasn't it, Lloyd?"

"No."

"What?"

"I mean, I don't know if he's dead. However

122

slight the chance, he may have escaped the mine alive and might be hunting us down."

"Forget it," Robinson said. "The man's dead."

"That's why I don't want anyone wandering outside. But I think you should go out looking, Robinson. Check the area, maybe ride into town to see if he shows there. I'd rather *know* he's alive than *think* he's dead. Of course, if you can get away with it, kill him. Don't take the time for a fight, don't shoot it out or have *fun* with him. Simply pump him full of hot lead and get him out of our lives. For good!"

Robinson smiled. "Great! Nothing I like better doing. Christ, I was worrying about you, Lloyd. Thought you'd turned soft. Guess I was wrong."

"Guess so."

Suzanna rose. "Why can't I go?"

The three men laughed.

"Damn it! Let me go and find him!"

"Christ, you'd probably suck him off instead of shoot him," Robinson said lasciviously.

Suzanna's cheeks burned, not out of embarrassment, or shock, but at the truthfulness of his statement. She'd probably do just that. She knew she couldn't kill the handsome man. She hadn't been able to do it before.

"See ya," Lloyd said to Robinson, who slapped Chuck's back and walked from the cabin.

"You never take me seriously," Suzanna said to Lloyd.

He shrugged. "No reason to."

Spur drank the last of the beer and turned toward the saloon's door. As he took a step a short, slightly overweight black haired man walked in. Spur instantly recognized him as Robinson, the one who'd jumped him from the tree. He didn't see Spur at first, so the Secret Service man turned his head and blended in with the men at the bar. From quick glances Spur saw Robinson look around the saloon while lingering in the door, then walk out.

Probably hunting me, Spur thought. He waited a good five seconds before hurrying toward the door and peering out. Robinson disappeared into the general store a second after Spur spotted him.

He left the saloon and stood in a shadow, waiting, watching. Robinson appeared again and Spur instantly turned away. Three seconds later he moved easily back around, half-expecting to see Robinson five feet from him. But the man simply entered another store, continuing his methodical if somewhat lackluster search.

Lloyd was being careful. Most men might have assumed that the cave-in had killed Spur. Maybe that's how Lloyd had kept in business so long—he was a thinker.

Robinson left the store and Spur suddenly realized one important fact—that *thinking man* had liberated his gun. He had no weapon.

Taking one last look at Robinson, Spur ducked into the general store and hastily asked for a Colt .45.

"What's your hurry, sir?" the cheery proprietor asked.

Spur grabbed the gun the man proffered, a box of ammunition, slapped the money down on the counter, then raced to the door, where he cautiously peered out.

Robinson turned and headed back toward Spur again. He pulled back from the window.

"I thought you were in a hurry," the jovial man said.

"Right," Spur countered. "Just don't want to be seen right now."

The man's face turned grave. "I don't want any trouble in my place," he said, pushing his hands out in front of him. "I've never had trouble in here, and I won't. Can't afford it. I'll charge you for any damage done."

"Fair enough," Spur looked out the window, then backed away from the door and ran to the counter.

"Just a minute!" the man said, a shotgun instantly in his hands as Spur raced around next to him. "You touch the money box and you're dead meat!"

"Don't want your money," Spur said. "Pretend I'm not here and your store will be fine." He hunched down out of sight behind the counter as he heard the door open and heavy footfalls cross the floor toward him.

"May I help you?" the shopkeeper asked, pretending he was inspecting the rifle.

"No," the voice said.

Spur recognized Robinson's growl.

"Then why are you here?" the clerk asked.

"Just lookin'," Robinson grunted.

"I see. Again."

Spur waited, quieting his breath, still crouched behind the wooden counter. Leave, Robinson. Just leave, damn you!

He kept the loaded Colt aimed directly up. If Robinson leaned over the counter the bastard'd be breathing dirt shortly. He should just kill him now, Spur thought.

But if he could remain undetected, he could follow the man back to the new hideout. Such an opportunity was too good to pass up, Spur knew.

He listened to Robinson's paces, following his movements from the noise: to the front of the store, to each side, probably to look out the windows, then back near the counter again.

Just a few more seconds.

The footsteps diminished in volume until they stopped momentarily. A door swung open and then slammed shut.

Spur started to rise, but thought better of it. Had Robinson left, or was he just trying to outthink him? Spur crawled two feet and peered from behind the counter. He saw the man's black boots and pants and then blasted a too fast shot at the surprised Robinson. The slug slammed into the wall as the shopkeeper yelled.

"No. No! Not in my store. Not in my store!"

Robinson ducked behind a molasses barrel and retured fire. Spur pounded a hole into the barrel, the thick goo inside stopping the bullet, then oozing out in a brown stream.

"Fifty pounds of molasses!" groaned the shopkeeper, who bent behind the counter and moved as far away from Spur as he could.

Spur waited until Robinson showed himself again and aimed at the fleeting hand. The blast boomed through the shop and slammed harmlessly into the door. Spur ducked back behind the counter and fired blind once. As he glanced to the door again he saw it was open.

Robinson was gone.

McCoy sprang to his feet and raced outside, ignoring the shopkeeper's complaints. Outside he checked every corner, every shadow. Nothing.

McCoy walked the length of the street, mimicking Robinson's earlier movements, he thought wryly, but didn't find him.

He cursed and set into a thorough search. He had an hour before the train arrived. It was the only one back to Cheyenne before the gold arrived there tomorrow, and Spur had to be on board before it rumbled through the dangerous zone.

Helena Fredrickson sat poised, stiff, drinking tea with Spur in the club car.

"A rattlesnake? Mine cave-in? A shootout in a general store?" She laughed. "Mr. McCoy, I'm surprised at you, making up such outlandish tales to explain your appearance." She clucked. "I've been riding back and forth, having them move my car each time I change directions, dealing with Mr. Mitchum's drinking and a woman who's about to give birth— and you've probably been out on a wild drinking spree and got caught up a fist fight. Am I right?"

Spur shook his head. "You asked me to let you know what I was doing. So that's what I've been doing, damn it! If you won't believe me I don't see why I should waste my time talking to you." He rose.

"No, wait," she said, then relaxed her shoulders. "I'm sorry, Spur. I'm just nervous about tomorrow. I guess I'm taking it out on you."

"Of course you are," Spur said. "Just don't let it affect your job performance."

She laughed. "I'm sorry. I begged Father—I

mean, I asked him not to allow the gold to be shipped tomorrow, but he wouldn't put it off. That's when I got the idea to help out with security. Right after that he asked you to protect it. That made me mad. I don't know why; maybe because I couldn't get him to do what I wanted. I'll admit it," she said smiling. "I'm spoiled. But at least I'm aware of it."

"So?"

"So?" she echoed.

Spur hesitated. "So it would be pleasant to see you smile once in a while, to hear you say something different than '*Mister* McCoy.' Hell, you know what it is, Helena? Maybe you should act more like a woman."

She looked at him, her soft blue eyes misting, then blinked and turned away. "I'll take that—under consideration."

"Good. So back to work." Spur didn't want to continue the talking about it when Helena was so close to crying. "That's what I know so far—there are five of them, three men, two women. I know their names and can describe them adequately. From what I heard the women don't actually participate in the robberies. They're more or less personal belongings of the men. I hope you don't find that too shocking."

"No. Not at all. Is there anything else?"

"Nothing I haven't already told you."

Helena rose. "Keep up the good work. I'll be around," she said, "if you need anything."

Spur nodded and watched the swaying motion of her slender hips as she walked up the club car aisle.

Suzanna started when the cabin door opened and slammed shut.

"Well?" Lloyd shouted.

"He's alive," Robinson said, panting.

"I knew it!" Suzanna said.

"Why didn't you kill him?"

"Couldn't get to him, and didn't want to give him a chance of following me. He wasn't budging, so I ducked out when I could, hid, then rode back here."

Lloyd's brows narrowed. "You sure he didn't follow you?"

Robinson stuck out his jaw. " 'Course I'm sure. What do you think I am?"

"He knows what you are," Suzanna interjected.

"Quiet, everybody!" Lloyd said, jabbing a finger in the air. "I have to think."

Suzanna went to Phoebe, who sat quietly still darning socks and sewing up holes in shirts.

"You don't seem too interested in this," Suzanna pointed out.

"I'm not. I couldn't care less. I just want out of here." Phoebe lowered her voice. "Now that we're in the cabin it'll be harder to leave. We can't just sneak out, and he won't let us go. He *needs* us—at least one of us—for the robbery," she whispered.

"To watch the horses," Suzanna said sullenly.

"That's right! You on watch tonight?"

She shook her head. "Last night."

"Darn. I guess we'll have to go through with it tomorrow—and then ride off afterward. We'll just get the first train and go anywhere!"

"All that money," Suzanna said. "I wish I could think of a way to make sure we get some of it."

Phoebe nodded. "We can't touch the old stuff, but this new money should be easy. We simply take a bag or two when we leave."

"What if he doesn't let us?"

Phoebe smiled. "We'll be poor. But if two good looking women alone in the west can't think of a way to make money, they just aren't trying hard enough."

"Phoebe! What are you saying?" she asked in delighted shock.

"Nothing. Nothing right now. We'll talk about this later."

"What are you two bitches yammering about?" Robinson asked in a loud voice.

"None of your business," Suzanna replied primly, then turned back to Phoebe.

The door banged open and Chuck Willis bounded into the cabin, out of breath.

"I saw something," he said, "when I was outside squatting."

"What was it?" Lloyd asked.

"A man on a horse. Comin' this way. He'll be here real soon."

CHAPTER THIRTEEN

Spur turned his cards over. "Twenty-one," he said.

The fat man across the table sneered at him. "Bull. You're cheating. You're pulling a fast one."

Spur's brows knotted as he looked at the man. They sat in the club car. "I don't cheat. I don't have to. I'm good at cards. And I don't like to be accused of cheating." He reached for the money in the center of the table, but his opponent pulled it to him first.

"It's mine! I should've won that hand. You're cheating! No one's that lucky!"

Spur admitted he had been fortunate—he'd won six out of six times. But he didn't like sore losers, even for half a dozen dollars.

"Are you going to hand over the money, or am I going to have to take it from you?"

The man smiled. He picked up the money and started counting.

Spur grabbed both his wrists and yanked them apart. The man howled in pain as he released the money which fluttered to the table. All conversation in the club car stopped and heads turned.

"Son of a bitch!" the man said, slurping his words in rage. "Not only a cheat, but a thief!"

"Cut the act. You lost. If you don't stop crying I'll give you a real reason to howl."

"Jesus, I'm scared," he said sarcastically. "Who the hell do you think you are? Taking the money I won from you?"

Spur stood. "Poor little bastard. Take the money if it means that much to you. I'll *give* it to you." Spur dumped it on his head.

"Son of a bitch!" the man sputtered. "Come back here!"

"Cheating at cards, now, Mr. McCoy?"

Spur heard Mitchum behind him. He turned and stuck a thumb back at the still whining man. "The guy can't seem to take losing."

Mitchum frowned. "How do I know you played fair? I wasn't there, and I don't know what kind of man you are, McCoy."

"I work for the government," Spur pointed out. "Who's word are you going to take—his or mine?"

The detective debated a moment. "Yours, I guess. But McCoy, don't rile up the passengers like that. It's not good for business when our employees cause fights in the club car."

"Yeah. Right." Spur looked at the man hard. "Any other suggestions?"

"N-n-no," he said.

"Then leave me alone." Spur walked off to make a tour of the train and found nothing out of the ordinary.

One more day. Tomorrow, when the No. 182

rolled into Cheyenne, he'd board it, talk with the express man, look over the gold, and then not relax for twenty-four hours until the treasure had safely passed through the dangerous region.

Spur was restless, wandering the cars, until he remembered Helena Fredrickson's smile. Damn good looking woman, he thought. If she wasn't the Union Pacific president's daughter he'd teach her a few things.

Lloyd looked out the window for signs of the approaching rider. Robinson sprang to the other window, facing south.

"You stupid bastard!" Lloyd said.

"Who?" Robinson asked.

"Who? You, goddamn it! You see him in town, but you don't kill him. And then you let him follow you right back here!"

"I didn't see the rider's face," Willis pointed out. "It might not be him."

"Who else would be riding around these parts? No one. Not anyone with any brains." Lloyd turned from the window and pulled the dusty, torn curtains closed, leaving them open a crack. "Get those other drapes over there shut," he yelled.

Robinson jerked them so hard they ripped.

"Still happy your man's alive?" Lloyd asked, flashing a look at Suzanna, who stood in the center of the cabin, holding Phoebe's hand.

"He's not my—oh, never mind. Besides, you don't know it's him."

"The hell I don't! But no matter who it is, he's about to get killed."

Phoebe's hands went over her ears. "I don't want

133

to hear it. I don't want to be here!"

"It's okay, Phoebe," Suzanna said. "I'll protect us." She grabbed the Colt from the table and knelt before the window beside Lloyd.

"What the hell do you think you're doing?" Lloyd asked, then knocked her away from him. "Get the hell out of my way, woman. This is man's work."

Suzanna cushioned her fall with her hands and came up beet-red. She clawed at his face with her fingernails, ripping downward, digging three furrows of blood down his cheek.

"Bitch!" he said, slapping her hand from his face. Lloyd pushed her so hard Suzanna stumbled back and fell on her bottom. "How many times do I have to tell you, woman?" he thundered.

"You beast!" Phoebe screamed, rushing to Suzanna. "How dare you?"

"Shh!" Willis said.

All five stopped and listened.

The pounding of the horse's hooves reached them from outside. Suzanna relinquished the weapon to Willis who, with a stern look, ran to crouch beside Robinson.

"Where?" Willis asked.

"I see him. Right in front of us," Lloyd whispered.

"At least he won't spot the horses," Robinson said as he moved to Lloyd's window.

"No. But he's seen the smoke."

The figure, still too distant to be seen clearly, halted his horse two hundred yards from the cabin. The animal whinneyed.

Lloyd saw the man dismount, then walk his horse into the trees. Damn him! Back to bother them again,

Lloyd thought. "He's out of sight—no, here he comes again."

The man appeared from a mass of trembling silver and green aspens. As he approached the cabin Lloyd was struck by the man's apparent lack of concern or fear. He appeared to be doing a natural thing.

The man moved closer and Lloyd let out a low whistle.

"What is it?" Suzanna asked.

"It's not the guy we had last night," Lloyd said.

"It isn't?" Suzanna said in joy.

"Hell, let's blast the fucker!" Robinson whispered.

Lloyd cracked the window open. At the movement the man halted two dozen yards from the cabin, then dashed behind a tree before Lloyd blasted two rounds into it.

"Shit! Missed him!" Robinson said thickly.

"You don't even know who he is!" Phoebe said, again covering her ears as she stood beside her sister. "Maybe he wasn't going to hurt us."

"Can't take that chance."

Robinson blasted the tree until it shook with the impact. "Whooee! Come on out of there, shitball! I need some live target practice."

"I can't see!" Willis complained, squirming in between the two men to look out the window.

Robinson slammed his elbow down hard on the boy's head. "Ain't nothing to see anyhow. Keep watch at the other window in case there's more than one of them."

Willis nodded and moved across the cabin.

Lloyd gazed at the tree; something was wrong. He

waited a few seconds, signalling Robinson to hold off shooting. Was the man still there?

"Lloyd!" Willis yelled as the glass above him shattered, arcing out against the curtains and falling to the floor in a clamour. Willis staggered back, rising to his feet.

"Get down! All of you!" Lloyd shouted while he rushed to the window and blasted two rounds into the area, then looked up. Smoke trailed up from a tree to his right; he reloaded while glancing at it, then ducked as a lump of hot lead sped above him.

"Too close," he said.

Willis stooped and moved to the center of the room. He shook his head; a tiny slice on his cheek bled slowly. He stared at Suzanna and Phoebe, dazed.

Robinson moved beside Lloyd and they pounded the tree, waiting for the man to make a mistake, or to run out of ammunition.

"Stop! Stop shooting! I can't stand it!" Phoebe screamed as she looked at the blood on Willis' cheek. She pressed her palms against her ears so hard that her knuckles turned white.

"Shut her up!" Robinson said with a look to Suzanna.

She held her sister, stroking her curly red hair, while the room filled with the odor of gunpowder and smoke.

"Just go ahead and kill him!" Suzanna said.

"Don't worry. We will." Lloyd's voice was determined.

The man suddenly ran from the tree toward another ten feet from it. Lloyd slammed two rounds at the man. The first plowed through his ribcage and drove into his spine, paralyzing him instantly. The

136

second went higher and lodged in his brain. He dropped limp to the ground as if his bones had turned to water.

Suzanna coughed at the sulphur odor and looked around when the explosions had died out.

"Is it over?" she whispered, staring at Lloyd hunched near the window, rifle in one hand, muzzle up. Smoke hung in the air, turning the room into a misty, dream-like scene.

"Yeah. That's it. He's dead."

Robinson swore, then pounded a round into the man's body. It jumped as the metal slammed into it. "Shit, Lloyd! You killed him. Why didn't you let me?"

"Robinson, shut the fuck up." Lloyd shook his head. "Do you think I care who the hell killed him? I just wanted him dead."

"Savages!" Phoebe said, releasing her ears from their finger prisons.

"Come off it, Lloyd!" Robinson said. "I know how you love to blow a man away. Shit, you almost get off doing it. I bet you popped a hard when you saw him drop."

"Would you shut your mouth, Robinson?" Suzanna said. "Talk about it later."

"I'll be later for you too, Suzanna," Lloyd said. "In fact, I don't see any reason not to tell you right now."

"Tell me what?" Suzanna demanded.

"I want you and your sister out of my gang. Permanently. You understand?"

"Nothing would suit us better," Suzanna said, glancing at Phoebe. "Isn't that the way you feel?"

She nodded.

"Good. We'll do the job tomorrow and then the next day you're on your own. You can ride into Pardo or wherever the hell you want—as long as you leave."

"We're not going anywhere until you pay us our share of the money."

Lloyd laughed. "You think it's that simple? That I can wander over to a bag and pull out the money? You know it's not here. I have to do some travelling, gather it up. I can't just hand it over."

"Then we'll stay here until you do," Suzanna said.

"But Suze, we—"

"No. We're staying." She avoided Phoebe's eyes.

Lloyd shrugged. "Fine. As long as you keep laying on your back for me, and Phoebe keeps cooking and sewing, you can stay. But if you ever get in my way again like you did today I'll boot both of you out. You nearly got us all killed."

"I was—only trying to help," Suzanna said.

"Some help," Willis chimed in.

"We don't need that kind of help." Robinson spat on the floor.

Lloyd walked out of the cabin cautiously to check the downed man, leaving the women and their problems behind him. The gunman was dead, all right. Half his face was gone, blown away, and gnats had already gathered to feast on the juices glistening on his exposed brain.

"He dead?" Robinson asked as he strode up to the body.

"Yeah. He won't bother us again."

"Look, Lloyd," Robinson said in a lowered voice. "Why wait until after the robbery tomorrow to get rid

138

of the girls? We have to move anyway—let's just leave them behind.''

''No way,'' Lloyd said. ''If we don't have their help tomorrow things will be harder.''

''We can do it without them,'' he said confidently.

''Would you like to stay with the horses?'' Lloyd asked, and turned before the flustered man could respond.

CHAPTER FOURTEEN

Spur made it back to Cheyenne at 6:00 that night, went to his hotel, ate and then slept until four. He splashed cold water on his face, dressed and walked through the dark town to the deserted train station. The iron horse wouldn't rumble through until 5:00, but he wanted some time to think.

His breath frosted the air before him in long clouds. Spur dug his hands into his coat pockets. Colder than usual this morning, he thought, watching dark clouds drift through the black sky. The wind picked up, cutting through his clothes and making him shiver. With the wind blew in a sprinkling of white powder.

Spur sat on his heels and fingered the stuff, which glowed softly in the intermittent moon and starlight. Snow. It was snowing in April.

Snow could change his plans. If it turned into a real blizzard the train could be snowbound. If he had to follow someone outside, the snow would both help and hurt him.

As he stood thinking about it, expecting the sky to open and flood down ice crystals, no more snow appeared. Just a fluke, he thought with a shrug, and returned to his planning.

The train pulled up. McCoy walked through the clouds of steam from the air brakes toward the first passenger car. The No. 182 had seven cars: three passenger, one club and dining, a private car, express car and caboose, plus an engine. The private car must be Helena Fredrickson's, Spur decided, if she were aboard. She might have given up her stupid idea of playing train detective and gone home. Spur hoped so.

As he climbed the steps a woman's voice greeted him.

"Mr. McCoy, how good it is to see you," Helena said above him.

Spur nodded. "Good morning, Miss Fredrickson."

"I trust you rested well?" She wore a black dress which, though fairly plain, showed the swell of her breasts and the curves of her hips.

"Yes, yes, I'm fine," he said as he stood beside her. "And you?"

"I love living on the rails!" she said. "As long as I have my private car I'll go anywhere. And I never sleep better than when I'm being lulled by the sway of the train."

"I see," he said, surprised at her exuberance. McCoy rubbed grit from his eye and stifled a yawn. "Excuse me, Miss Fredrickson, but I have to work."

"Just a minute." She laid a hand on his shoulder as he turned to leave. "I think we should talk over our strategies."

"Strategies?"

"Yes. You know, what to do in case of a robbery."

Spur didn't attempt to hide his frown. "Miss Fredrickson, if there *is* a robbery I'd suggest you keep your pretty head down and let me handle it."

Her cheeks colored. "I see. I wasn't referring to myself personally," she said proudly. "I'm discussing the passengers. Should an announcement be made?"

Spur shook his head. "You don't seem to understand. A train robbery isn't like a church social. If we get boarded by men with guns I'm sure the passengers will be able to figure out what's happening. Now good morning, Miss Fredrickson." He turned and walked past her to the express car.

Leaving a shocked Helena behind him, Spur made his way through the passenger cars. The oil lamps were turned down low and most of the passengers attempted to sleep. They slumped uncomfortably on the hard seats, some propped up on pillows, with legs and arms dangling into the aisle. Most of the passengers were male.

He walked quietly among them through two cars and then through one Pullman, its berths curtained off. Nothing seemed amiss.

A sleepy man in a white apron stood behind a polished wood bar in the club car, sipping coffee from a cracked china cup. Spur went through the deserted car and then reached Helena Fredrickson's coach. He either had to walk through it or over it to reach the express car. Hell, Spur thought—he needed to get his blood pumping this morning anyway.

On the vestibule he looked up at the top of Helena's car, gripped a handle placed near the roof, and climbed. McCoy threw a leg on the roof, hauled himself up, and then stood slightly bent.

He walked down the roof with measured steps, sensitive to the train's slightest movements beneath him. When Spur reached the end he climbed down and walked across the connector to the express car.

Spur knocked slowly on the door twice, paused and knocked again. The pre-arranged signal allowed the express man to know that his visitor had arrived. Normally all the knocking a person could do wouldn't make him open the door—not unless it was a regularly scheduled one.

A surly face peered at Spur from behind the partially opened door as he looked up at it. The man summed up McCoy.

"Yeah?" he said.

"Vincent Glass?" Spur asked.

"Yeah. Who're you?"

"Spur McCoy."

The man relaxed. "Okay, come on in, Mr. McCoy. I've gotta get this door shut."

Spur walked inside the warm car, thankful that its oil heater was lit. He stopped beside Glass.

"This here's the baggage, cargo and freight area. The back half, there, that's the postal area."

Spur saw canvas bags hanging from racks, countless four-inch square doors with drawers behind them. He nodded. "Where's the gold?"

"I'm getting to that," Glass said, and frowned.

The man was so thin his clothes seemed to wear him. His face was numb with continuous danger and boredom, teeth uneven and tobacco stained, and his face perpetually flushed as if he secretly drank while locked within the car at work.

"How long ago did the Union Pacific hire you?" Spur asked as he studied the man.

"Two months ago," Glass said glumly. He moved with slumped shoulders toward four inconspicuous safes sitting on the floor—two-foot square boxes. "There's your gold. All $200,000 worth of it." He shook his head. "I'm trying hard not to think about all that money—it might make a man nervous."

"Sure would. You don't know the safe's combinations, do you?"

"Nope, and I don't want to. I don't even want to see it."

"Good. Keep this car tight until we reach San Francisco."

The man nodded. "Of course! That's what I'm paid for. But I'm getting off at Selton—a new express man comes on."

"Just make sure the gold doesn't leave with you," he said with a smile.

Glass looked at him strangely, suspiciously, his eyes narrowed. "What kind of talk is that?"

"Just a joke, okay?" Spur said. "It's nothing." He smiled. "Thanks for the look around, Glass. I hope we don't have any trouble."

"No thanks are due," he said with a shrug. "I just do what they tell me. Besides, it breaks up the monotony." He ran his palm across his forehead. "Sometimes I think I'll go crazy locked in here for six hours at a time."

"Just don't do it today," Spur said.

The man frowned. "Another joke?"

"Right." Spur turned and waited for Glass to unlock the door. The man shuffled forward and did so without comment.

As he went into the next car he forgot it belonged to Helena. He walked in, shivering from the chill outside—and was shocked to see Helena Fredrickson standing before him. He smiled as he took in the picture.

Helena stood lacing up her corset behind her, bent over, her exposed breasts hanging down. Black silk stockings held up by black garters completed her attire. She looked at him in surprise, then mild amusement as he walked closer.

"I *am* disappointed in you, Mr. McCoy," she said, finished tying a knot. "I didn't figure you were the type of man who'd walk into a woman's private coach, hoping to catch her in an undressed state." She planted her hands on her hips, not trying to cover her breasts.

Spur returned the banter, since the woman didn't seem particularly surprised or shocked. "You're not undressed. Not quite."

"Are you disappointed? Sorry, but I'm cold. I'm afraid this show is over." She slipped on a chemise, stepped into two lace-edged petticoats, then the black dress he'd previously seen her in. "I know some men enjoy seeing women dressed in their underthings. Are you one of them?"

"Depends."

"On what?"

"On the woman."

She laughed. "Would you help me?" Helena said, turning her back.

"Sure." He buttoned her up.

"You wouldn't have caught me like this if I hadn't tied my corset too tight this morning. It's hard enough to do it by myself, but on a moving train it's nearly impossible."

He finished the last button. "If you ever need help again, Miss Fredrickson, I'll be happy to assist."

"Maybe I'll call you." She turned. "I figured you'd be willing to come to my aid. Now if you'll excuse me, Mr. McCoy, you should be going back to work and I should finish dressing."

"Fine."

"But don't go just yet. Were you in the express car just now?"

"Yes. Why?"

"I was wondering. Did you—did you see the gold?" She looked at him hurriedly, then glanced away.

Spur caught her curious tone. What was Helena up to? "No, just the safes."

"Oh." She seemed relieved.

"Why?"

"Because—because I couldn't see it either. I tried, but the express man wouldn't even let me into the car."

Spur suppressed a smile.

"Never mind," Helena said. "I don't care. One more question—is this the first time you've passed through here?"

"Yes. I walked overhead on my way to the express car. Why? Did you hear me?"

"No. It was—never mind." She shook her head.

"I'm sorry I surprised you just now."

"Don't be. I kind of enjoyed it." She smiled and flicked her tongue invitingly over her lips. "You can come through my car any time, Spur McCoy. Or you could just come visit me—when the gold's out of danger, of course."

"Of course. I'll consider it," Spur left her, his nose still full of the heady perfume with which she'd splashed herself.

"You *what?*" Lloyd thundered, slamming his coffee cup down on the table.

"You heard me!" Suzanna hissed. "You can't talk me out of this. Not this time, Ray Lloyd!"

"Goddamn bitch!" Robinson rose from his chair.

"Why the hell should I help out in your robbery when I know I'll never see a cent from it? What makes you think I'm that stupid?"

"Look, Suzanna," Phoebe began.

"Stay out of this, Phoebe!" Lloyd roared. "Come on, Suzanna. I'm counting on you." His eyes held hers.

She looked away from them, but turned back, remembering the times he'd taken in her untamed animal lust. She recalled the mysterious, wild side of the man that had captivated her, and remembered his maleness sliding down between her legs.

"No!" she said, shaking off the feelings and memories. "I won't watch the horses for you. And I won't be part of this stupid robbery of yours unless you let me be right there with you—helping you out." She paused. "Don't think you'll get Phoebe to hold the horses. You won't do it, will you, Phoebe?" She didn't look at her sister.

"No," Phoebe said quietly.

"Damn the both of you!" Robinson said. "We can't carry that much gold, not with just two of us on the train."

"What're we going to do?" Willis asked.

"Everyone shut up!" Lloyd thundered. After a few seconds, he spat. "We can't do it without them," he said to Robinson.

"You're damned right you can't!" Suzanna said.

"But we certainly can't do it with Suzanna around either."

"I think you're going to have to," she said. "Either that or leave some of the gold behind. You won't do that, will you, Ray? You never leave any behind."

"And you're betting that he'll even put up with you to get that gold," Robinson said slowly.

"It's too late to call in any help," Suzanna pointed out.

"I'm not going to let you fuck up this robbery! And I won't hang because some dumb cunt wants to play train robber." He shook his head, slammed his fist down on the table. "We won't go."

"What?" Robinson blurted out. "Jesus Christ, Lloyd! You're going to let her blow our chances for two hundred thousand dollars! A job like this'll never come around again. So what if she can't shoot or ride or do nothing but spread her legs? Let's just stick her in the background and do it."

"What if I disguise myself as a man and never talk?" Suzanna asked, excitement lighting her eyes. "I'll stay out of the way, watching for trouble. You, Steve and Chuck can do all the dirty work. I don't know anything about blasting safes, or robberies, but I can be a lookout." She paused. "Come on, Lloyd. You know you can't pass up this robbery."

"No!" Lloyd thundered.

"Now you listen, Lloyd!" Robinson roared. "I'd

do this job with the kid myself if I could, but we have to do it together or not at all. And I'm not going to watch you piss away this chance. Let's do it. I never thought I'd say this, damn it, but let her tag along."

"Who'd watch the horses?" Willis called out before Lloyd could respond.

"Phoebe," Suzanna said, pointing to her sister, who stood in a corner.

She looked at Suzanna in alarm. "What? No. I can't! I'd do it wrong! All I do is cook, sew and wash."

"You don't have to worry," Suzanna said, walking to her and draping an arm around Phoebe's shoulders. "You simply ride with the horses for a mile at the most and wait for us there—hidden. Really, it's not much different from riding at home."

"But I'm scared!" Phoebe said, her eyes round with fear.

"She can't do it," Lloyd said. "She won't be there with the horses."

"Yes she will. Won't you, Phoebe?" Suzanna stared hard at her sister.

Phoebe gazed at her for a moment, then screwed up her face and nodded stubbornly.

"Well," Lloyd said.

"And you'll hand over our two-fifths of the share of this robbery as soon as we make it back here!" Suzanna demanded.

"Hold on, woman!" Lloyd said. "I never agreed to that stupid little plan!"

"Lloyd, it's either that or nothing," Robinson said quietly.

"Will you hang back and keep out of my fucking way, obey my orders without questions?" Lloyd asked.

"Yes!" Suzanna said, staring at him.

Lloyd's frown deepened, then he shook his head. "Fuck. It'd be a shame to pass up that gold." A pause. "Okay. We'll all go—and Phoebe'll watch the horses."

Suzanna cheered. Robinson grinned hesitantly. Willis and Phoebe looked blank, and Lloyd's face was quiet. He turned to the window.

"I may regret this, but there's no way out."

He's just mad that I got my own way, Suzanna thought. She had turned things around, made him see her point, and talked him into it. An incredible feeling boiled up inside her, then spread throughout her body and threatened to burst out. In her jubilation she looked at Phoebe, whose eyes were dark. Suzanna almost thought she saw her sister's lips trembling.

Lloyd turned back to Suzanna. "Don't think just because you boxed me into this that I think you're any better than any woman. You're not. I don't approve of women doing anything but spreading their legs, having babies, and taking care of the house." He frowned. "But if it's the only way I'll get my hands on that gold—and if it'll show you just how wrong you are —fine. You'll come along. Just don't get us all killed."

Suzanna smiled. "They'll never know I'm a woman," she said, shaking her head. "As long as no one talks to me, I'll be fine."

Lloyd sighed. "Why'd I ever get mixed up with women again?" he asked Robinson, who slapped his back and smiled.

Suzanna glanced at Phoebe again, and saw the barest suggestion of a brave smile break out over her face.

CHAPTER FIFTEEN

The 182 thundered around a curve in the forested, mountainous terrain. Its diamond-shaped stack belched smoke into the sky while slicing across the landscape.

Inside, Spur McCoy paced in the club car, impatient. He stopped to look out the window. The tracks turned in the distance and then angled sharply upward, climbing one half foot every two feet. Snow lay on the ground at the higher elevations.

That's the dangerous area, Spur thought, leaning against the frigid glass to look closer. Not much else to see outside—trees, clouds hanging in the huge sky, and bushes, but something else *was* out there—Lloyd, Robinson and Willis were waiting for the train. Even though Spur had found them and escaped, and in spite of the fact that they knew the Union Pacific had been warned of possible attack, Spur was sure Lloyd wasn't a man to back down on a plan. The robbery would occur.

He wandered back to the club car, accepted a cup

of coffee from the bored barman, and stood sipping it.

"Slow morning," he said to the barkeep.

"Always slow this time of morning. Say, aren't you that new detective they hired on?"

Spur was surprised by the question. "What makes you think that?"

The man shrugged. "Just wondering. I heard someone talking about you."

"Maybe."

"Say, we're not in any real danger, are we?" He looked around quickly. "I mean, you don't think we'll be robbed or anything. Huh?"

"Can't say," Spur said. "I don't know. But the Union Pacific seems worried."

"Worried enough to hire you?" the barman asked.

Spur shrugged.

"It's enough to make a man want to get off this train."

"You nervous?" Spur asked.

"Yes," he said flatly. "And I don't mind admitting it. That doesn't mean I can't hold my own in a gunfight—but we're not allowed to wear one at work."

"Don't worry. It's bad for the heart."

"Thanks for the advice," the barman said, smiling.

Spur drained his cup and set it on the bar. He moved from the club car into the vestibule between it and Helena's private coach. As the chill air hit him Spur was struck by its ferocity. He looked up at the sky and watched black and gray clouds boil overhead, threatening to spill momentarily.

It might snow after all. He stepped back into the

club car and stared at the private car from the warmth inside. He wondered what Vincent Glass, the express man, was thinking now. Was he bored, or nervous?

The train slowed considerably, and Spur checked out the window to investigate. Robbers, Indians, a missing section of track? Maybe too much snow? He couldn't see anything to his right so he looked out the other side.

A second track was laid along the rails and a reserve engine sat puffing. There's the extra power to push the train over the hills, Spur thought. The 182 moved over to the ancillary track and Spur could imagine the switchman pushing one end of the link through the iron drawbar of the first engine, and then thrusting an iron spike through the drawbar, then repeating the entire process with the other end of the link in the 182's engine. Seconds later the whistle shrieked and they were once again underway.

Spur started his circle tour of the train as it bit at the hill, steadily decreasing in speed despite the added engine. As the train continued to climb, the grade increased and their progress slowed even more. Finally the train ground down to a five mile-an-hour speed. Spur knew he could hop off the train, walk beside it, then jump back on. Never having ridden on this part of the track, Spur hadn't fully known how dangerous it was. No wonder the Lloyd gang had chosen the spot.

Spur looked out at the trees and rocks that passed by, now covered with snow. As he did, the train seemed to lose slightly more speed. He started to sweat.

Where the hell are you, Lloyd? he thought. Come and get me. I'm ready.

* * *

Helena Fredrickson felt the train slow and her heart raced. This was it. If she could keep her head, walk among the passengers, act as if nothing could possibly happen, and above all avoid any direct confrontation with the robbers if they did indeed show, she'd be fine. Then she could travel on to Sacramento, or return home sooner, having fulfilled her dreams.

She fumbled with an earring that threatened to fall again, then checked her appearance in the mirror. Her ample black dress seemed appropriate for the occasion, and she was pleased at the picture she saw.

Helena straightened a lock of hair that had gone awry, then smiled into the mirror and went to the door. Outside her private car, she closed the door behind her, shivered in the cold, and walked quickly into the club car.

Without thinking Helena searched the car for Spur McCoy. When she realized what she was doing, Helena laughed. Why are you looking around for him? she asked herself. Because you like the way he looks, and acts? Or because you'll feel safer if he's beside you?

She shook off the thoughts and walked among the passengers asking if they were comfortable and glancing nervously out the windows every opportunity she had. The scenery outside, blanketed with snow, slanted at an obvious angle, impressing even more strongly in her mind the robbery's possible immediacy. If they were going to be robbed it would happen along this stretch of tracks. The thought wasn't comforting.

Helena caught her foot on a man's leg and stumbled.

"Careful," a young man said, rushing up to catch her from falling. As he did so his hand brushed against her breasts.

"I'm sorry, lady. Didn't you see my leg?"

"No, I didn't," she said.

"Hey, are you all right?" the fresh faced youth asked.

"Yes. Really." She straightened her hair and continued on into the next car, embarrassed at the scene she'd caused.

Calm down! she told herself.

"Are you coming!" Lloyd yelled from his horse into the cabin.

"Just a minute!" Suzanna called out. She turned to Phoebe. "Are you sure you're going to be fine?"

Phoebe looked down. "I—I guess so."

"There's nothing to worry about, Phoebe. I've done it lots of times. I've never seen a gun pulled or a railroad detective show or nothing. By the time Lloyd and the others get back to you and the horses, they'll have the money and all you've got to do is make sure none of the horses run off. You can do that, can't you?"

"Jesus Christ!" Lloyd yelled. "We've got to go. Now!"

"Okay!" Suzanna called. "Come on. We can't hold up the others!"

The two women bundled up their coats and walked outside. Snow fell softly.

She climbed up onto her horse and waited until

Phoebe was mounted as well, then turned to Lloyd. "Let's go," she said briskly.

Lloyd ignored her and turned his horse toward the tracks.

"Phoebe, see the snow? It's a lucky sign."

She shrugged. "Is that what it is?"

"Of course. What else could it mean?"

Phoebe frowned. "I don't know. I keep thinking about the government man."

"Well don't!" Suzanna said. Lloyd looked at her from his usual forward position. "Even if he does try to stop the robbery," she continued, ignoring Lloyd's inquiring glance, "I don't think he's the kind of man who'd kill a woman."

"But I heard that women were hung out here. Legally!"

"Only stupid bitches who talk too much," Robinson said, leaning back to them.

"Ignore him," Suzanna said. "You know what women are in the west! We're like priceless objects that men pass around among themselves. And they don't waste us like that!"

"So I shouldn't be worried?"

"No."

"I'll try not to be."

Snow flurried as Suzanna smiled at her sister, but trembled—not only from the cold, or the flakes that clung to her cheeks like feathers. She was scared. In fact, she couldn't remember ever having been so terrified—not of any man, animal, even of God.

They rode on through the rocky area, their horses' sure hooves finding holds on the sloping, snowy terrain. As they rounded another hill Suzanna saw the tracks stretched out before her. She rode up beside Lloyd, who looked at her with irritation.

"What the hell do you want?"

"Where's the train?" she asked excitedly.

"Somewhere in the east. If we could see it from here we'd already be late."

"Oh." She slowed her horse until it came into step beside Phoebe's mount. The snow was lighter now, still sticking to the ground save where the wind blew it into drifts which stacked up near trees and rocks. Suzanna shivered again from the deep cold that penetrated her layers of clothing. As she rode on Suzanna dreamt of theatre openings in Sacramento, fine wines and a mansion at the very top of Nob Hill.

Ten minutes later Lloyd halted them near the tracks. The men dismounted, then Suzanna followed suit. Lloyd looked up at Phoebe as he handed her the reins to the other horses.

"See that cliff over there?" he said, pointing to a spot a mile distant down the tracks.

She nodded. "Yes."

"There's a hollow there, right beneath it, with a clump of trees. Wait for us there. Don't go anywhere, and don't take the horses anywhere. No matter how cold it gets. You understand me, woman?"

"Yes, but—"

"There are no buts," Lloyd said.

"What if the snow falls three feet thick?"

"Don't move. We'll worry about that later," Lloyd said with a glance at the dark sky.

Suzanna kissed her sister's forehead, pulled her hat more snugly around her face, and smiled. "See you soon," she said.

Suzanna waved as she and the men, bundled against the howling wind and blasting snow, set off to

159

walk the last few hundred feet to the train tracks. The snow wasn't more than a sprinkling on the ground yet so the walk wasn't difficult, but Suzanna found herself stumbling over things that weren't there, and she had to forcefully will herself to calm down.

Robinson noticed her slips and snorted. "She's scared," he said to Lloyd.

"Yes, a little," Suzanna said defiantly. "Aren't you?"

"No."

Suzanna steeled herself. "Take care of yourself, Steve, and I'll worry about me," she said as harshly as she could manage.

Robinson laughed.

Suzanna looked at Lloyd. He frowned and moved on in front of her.

"You'll be fine, Suzanna," he said, without looking at her, "just keep in the background and don't say anything." He turned his head and pointed at her bosom. "Can you still use that thing?"

"You mean my derringer?" She nodded. "Sure. I practice once in a while."

"Don't do any *practicing* today. Remember— never point your gun at a man unless you plan to shoot him, and never shoot a man unless you plan to kill him."

"I know that!" Suzanna said quickly.

The four moved toward the tracks across the snow-blown countryside. As the whistle blew in the distance, Suzanna felt her heart stop momentarily.

CHAPTER SIXTEEN

The forest around her smelled wet. Suzanna followed the male gang members from the wooded area to a gigantic boulder situated near the tracks. She calmly told herself that this was a dream, and that she didn't have to live through it. Suzanna shut off her fears and anxieties and switched to instinct and reflex.

"How you feel?" Willis asked as they squatted behind the boulder.

"Just fine," Suzanna said too forcefully. Then she shrugged. "Hell, Chuck, I'm scared to death."

"I know. I was too the first time."

"But this'll be the only time for me!"

"You're goddamned right it is!" Robinson bellowed.

"Cut the talk!" Lloyd said as the grind of metal against metal screamed across the area. "It's almost here. Places, everyone!"

Suzanna moved to the left side of the boulder, where she stood next to Willis. Suzanna's appearance had altered drastically from the everyday: she'd tucked her hair under her hat and pulled its brim low over her forehead. Suzanna had dressed in a white cotton shirt, vest, black leather jacket, and denim jeans cut too big for her so that her curves wouldn't show. From a distance, and even up close to someone who didn't know her, Suzanna Buckland could indeed be mistaken for a man.

She hoped she wouldn't meet any handsome men on the train, then told herself she didn't care what anyone thought when they saw her—she was after gold and adventure. Suzanna had to act and look tough and keep her mouth shut.

She glanced back at Lloyd, who crouched on the other side of the boulder.

"Now?" she asked impatiently as she listened to the train roar up.

"Yes!" Lloyd called. He rushed from the boulder, with Robinson not far behind.

"Come on!" Willis yelled behind him as he also disappeared.

For one agonizing second Suzanna stood poised, not knowing whether to move or even that she could move. Then she found strength and willed her legs to propel her around the huge rock and toward the now slowly passing train. She had to run faster to catch up with the others; they were already on board, ten feet up the line.

She made it there easily and pulled herself up onto the stairs and the vestibule without the men's help. Lloyd looked around, then reached for the door.

Helena Fredrickson, standing in the first of three passenger cars, glanced out the window and was astonished to see three figures emerge from a boulder as the train passed by. She shot to her feet and ran out the car into the next one, searching for Spur. Had he seen them? Could they be the robbers?

Helena rushed through the last passenger car and came to the club car. She stopped before crossing the vestibule to go in, though—she saw four figures at the rear of the car through the window.

"Spur, where *are* you?" Helena called as she backed away from the windows, unable to enter the car. Were those the robbers?"

Then she shook her head. No. She wouldn't give in to fear. She had to find out what was going on in the car.

Helena lifted her chin and marched from the passenger car and out onto the vestibule, then straight into the club car.

Spur sat at the rear of the club car, figuring that with five cars to cover, the club was the best, since it was closest to the gold. He didn't worry whether Lloyd and his gang would rob the passengers—with $200,000 in easy cash on the express car, Spur knew Lloyd wouldn't be after gold watches and old ladies' lockets.

Since he was one coach distant from the express car Spur rose periodically to check it. He'd been to the express car twice so far, travelling over Helena's coach—not an easy job with wind and snow to contend with.

The train continued to groan up the hill as Spur stubbed out his cheroot in the silver ashtray and rose. Might as well check the express car again, he thought, just to give him something to do. Spur was bursting with nervous energy, itching to do something. Anything!

As he rose four men moved from the bar together toward the passenger cars. Spur walked to the door and opened it, then glanced through the curtains to Helena's car. He didn't relish the thought of climbing over it again, so he continued on into it. He walked through the spacious car, filled with frilly lampshades, toss pillows, teak furniture, and even a small chandelier that constantly swayed with the train's movement. He went on. When he was three feet from the door it burst open. A short man with his face covered with a mask rushed into the room. Robinson.

Spur dove behind a table and fired.

Robinson bolted into a closet and returned the shot. Expensive mirrors and pieces of crystal shattered as the man shot aimlessly at Spur.

"Come on out of there, fucker!" Robinson said. "I don't like having to flush out assholes like you."

Spur puncutated the air with a shot as the closet door opened a crack. It splintered the door. Since Robinson was out of sight, Spur decided to try a new angle.

"What's the matter, Robinson, you scared? I always knew you were yellow. Why are you hiding?"

Robinson grunted. "Why are you?"

"You're scared. You're afraid to shoot it out with me face to face, man to man. You know why you're scared?"

"I'm not scared, damnit!"

"Because you know I'm faster than you. I'm faster and better. I can outdraw nine out of ten men who go up against me," Spur said, exaggerating slightly.

"Yeah?" Robinson snorted. "I guess I'm that tenth man."

"No way. You're yellow. I'm surprised the women even let you touch them. You're not even a real man."

"You bastard! No one calls me that!" Robinson cracked open the door and blasted another round in Spur's general direction.

"Come on, Robinson. A fair fight. You and me alone. A showdown."

"Sure. And I'm supposed to walk out there first? You'd gun me down in a second. I'm not that stupid."

"No I won't. I'm a man of my word."

"Bullshit!"

Spur smiled. "We'll go at the same time."

Neither man moved.

The door behind Spur opened.

"Get down!" he yelled.

He heard a woman's scream as Robinson opened the closet door and looked out. Spur's muzzle lined up perfectly with the fat man's chest and shot a sterile bullet into his body, ripping through his upper chest and pushing out his back.

"Spur!" a woman's voice called.

"Helena. What the hell are you doing here?" he said, still watching Robinson, who lay on his back, a dark red stain on his light coat.

"I—I was coming to warn you," she said, gasping.

"Get in a corner and hide yourself, or get the hell out of here!" Spur yelled. Robinson stirred then, reaching for the pistol that lay just out of his reach.

"Don't do that," Spur said. "You touch that gun and you're dead."

The man groaned, dragged his other hand up to touch the wound, and wetted his fingers in his own blood. "Jesus Christ!" Robinson said, shock suffusing his face. "You've shot me!"

"Yeah," Spur said thickly.

Robinson arched his back. His body jacknifed with pain as he let out a howl and his arms jerked on the floor. "You son of a bitch! No one's ever shot me. Christ, it burns. Burns like fire!"

"Go ahead and roll around in it," Spur said. "This is your chance to visit the hell that all your victims went through when you shot them."

Helena's plush car, now a mass of broken silvered glass and hole-ridden drapes, rang with Robinson's screams. The man gyrated on the ground.

"Relax, Robinson," Spur said. "You're not gonna die from that wound—not unless you make me shoot you again. Keep your mouth shut."

"Kill me then, you fuckin' bastard! I'll never go to jail, and I'll never hang!"

Before Spur could respond to the challenge the door behind Robinson opened and a masked blond haired man blasted as he came into the room. Spur returned fire as he ducked behind a couch, glancing at Robinson as he went down. The man lay motionless, though his eyes stared up at the ceiling, sightless with the depths of unconsciousness.

"Robinson!" Willis cried as he saw his friend lying on the floor.

Spur blasted a bullet as the man ducked, punching a hole through Willis' hat brim.

"Robinson!" said the boy. "What should I do?"

Spur was dimly aware of movement behind him as he tried to get a clean shot at the boy. "Get down!" he yelled, thinking that Helena had stirred from her hiding place. But an explosion behind him told him that it wasn't Helena who had moved.

"McCoy!" Mitchum said. "Thanks for calling me to help." Mitchum's voice was followed by several blasts in succession from his six-gun.

Despite Spur's lack of faith in the man's abilities, Mitchum was certainly handy with a weapon. As he reloaded Spur watched Mitchum's aim steadily increase in accuracy. Finally just as Spur rejoined the fight Mitchum's bullet bored a hole through Willis' forehead as he looked up to fire. The young man's eyes crossed and he sighed as his body slumped to the ground.

"Took care of those two, didn't we?" Mitchum asked, his face flushed with excitement as he looked at Spur.

"Helena? Are you still there?" he called, ignoring Mitchum's enthusiasm.

She rose. "Yes, I'm fine."

"Run, don't walk out of here. Go now!" Spur said. "And don't look back here."

"What? Why not?" She turned and looked. Her hand went to her mouth and Helena gasped.

"Get her out of here," he said to Mitchum. "I'm going after the others." He hurried toward the door.

"Spur, goddamn you!" Mitchum yelled. "You can't make me stay back here!"

"No time to argue," he said. "Get her to safety and join me."

The train continued to grind slowly up the hill as Spur raced from Helena's private car toward the express car. As he looked out the door windows he saw Lloyd and another masked figure at the door of the express car. Swearing, Spur opened the door. As it swung inward Lloyd looked at Spur, took a hasty shot and dove off the train into a three-foot thick snow pack that had been pushed up by the trains next to the track. The other figure darted past Spur, trying to shove him over the low railing. He was surprisingly weak for a man, he thought, following him into Helena's car. Spur fired at the fleeing figure through the opened door, then slid back out of range. He looked in Helena's car again and saw a returning Mitchum squeeze off a shot.

The figure gave out a sharp cry and fell gracefully to the ground. Suspicious, Spur watched and his mouth opened in wonder as the hat fell off, releasing a cascade of straight red hair that settled around its head on the floor. Suzanna Buckland, Spur thought, though he couldn't see her face.

"My God!" Mitchum said. "It's a woman! McCoy, I swear I never would have shot her if I—"

"There's no way you could have known," Spur said sadly, shaking his head. "She must be dead."

"What's next?" Mitchum asked.

"Stop the train," he said. "I'm leaving."

"Where?" he asked suspiciously.

"I'm going to follow the guy who jumped off the train—Lloyd, the gang's leader."

Spur hurried out and then down the steps and leaped toward a sea of white crystals, knowing Lloyd was out there—somewhere.

CHAPTER SEVENTEEN

As Spur hit the snowbank he blinked but felt no impact. His feet, propelled by the jump, continued on for a foot and a half through the hard packed snow. His cheeks and hands ached with cold as he shook his head and tried to stand. The snow started to support him, only to give way. Finally he reached the ground and pushed his upper body out of the snow.

Spur glanced around. Where was Lloyd? He'd probably headed back for the train. Spur couldn't see him, but that didn't mean much—the man might be running beside the train. Besides, snow was falling and that hampered visibility.

Spur tried to walk. The snow pushed back at him, resisting. He kicked and scooped it out from before him and eventually made it out of the snowbank. He cursed as he stumbled over the tracks and hurried down them, toward the rapidly departing train, shivering in the near zero temperature.

Spur wondered if Lloyd had already made it back

on the train. If so, he hoped Mitchum would take care of him.

Mitchum, the man who shot women—who'd killed beautiful Suzanna.

As soon as he dropped off the train, Lloyd turned and his long legs moved swiftly as he ran beside the train. If the third to the last car was a private coach, then the next one had to be the express car, Lloyd rationalized.

From what he could see through the open door as he neared it, both Robinson and Willis were dead. He had no idea what had happened to Suzanna after he'd jumped off, and didn't want to think about it. No time. He could still blow the safe's door, get inside and take the money.

He hopped onto the connector between the cars and saw Suzanna lying on the floor face down in the plush private car, surrounded by the luxury she had craved.

Suzanna Buckland—dead.

Ray Lloyd turned to the door of the express car, then carefully unwrapped a stick of dynamite. Just one would be enough. He hastily wedged it between the express car's handle and the door, lit a match in cupped hands, and held it to the fusetip. It caught and burst into a bright sizzling point of light which slowly burned up the fuse.

The wind chill howled around him and the snow level descended to his knees as Spur continued running toward the train. The steep incline, dangerous weather and snow blowing into his eyes combined to make the short trip a taxing one. Why hadn't Mitchum stopped the train by now? Surely the engineer knew something was wrong. The train puffed fifty feet from him, still moving slowly up the sharp hill.

He powered into his run through the foot of snow. Spur's feet shook with cold; the snow had melted against his warm skin and run down into his boots.

Spur ran toward the train, half slipping with each step but balancing as he strode over the snow. It continued to fall and blow around him, adding to the already growing mass on the ground. Hopefully he wouldn't have to be out in it again, Spur thought.

He ran along the tracks where the train's passing had cleared much of the snow lying on them. Pain cut into his lungs as he inhaled the frigid air.

Spur made it to the caboose but continued running to the right side, past the red painted car. He jumped onto the vestibule between the caboose and express cars and looked at the door. Of course it was locked, and Spur had no way of knowing if Lloyd was already inside. He wearily glanced at the ladder extending to its roof and started up it.

Atop the express car Spur found his balance in a crouch, then stood and walked slowly across it. Halfway there Spur heard an explosion which rocked the car. As glass shattered somewhere Spur's feet slipped on the snow covered roof. He scrambled for balance but not before gravity had taken control of his body. He rolled off the roof and fell twenty feet into a snow bank. Spur felt new flakes landing on his face as he shook his head, the wind knocked out of him.

Lloyd had dynamited the express car's door, Spur thought. Or had it been the safes?

He pushed out from the snow drift, thankful that

he hadn't fallen on hard rock, and ran toward the train which still continued on away from him. Why the hell hadn't Mitchum stopped the damn thing yet?

"No you don't!" a voice said behind him.

Mitchum glanced around in alarm. He'd just walked into the private car on his way to find Spur when the voice stopped him.

The *dead* red haired woman had suddenly revived herself. She sat on the floor, apparently unharmed, a derringer in her hand.

Mitchum held his Colt steady.

"You wouldn't want to hurt a woman, would you?" she asked Mitchum, licking her lips.

"No," he said, confused. "I—I t-though you were d-d-dead," he said.

"No. I just know when to lay down on the floor and *pretend* I'm dead." She smiled and rose slowly to her feet, never dropping her aim with the wicked little weapon. "Actually, I didn't know if anyone was around, and couldn't find out without opening my eyes and sitting up. But you're the bastard who shot at me, aren't you?"

"That's right," he said. "But I didn't know you were a woman!"

Suzanna looked outside, then back at the man. "What's your name?"

"Mitchum. James Mitchum." He was confused; Mitchum knew he couldn't shoot the woman. What should he do?

"Mine's Suzanna. Well, James, it's like this." She stopped speaking and moved closer to him. "Won't you put that thing away?" she asked, gesturing at his pistol with her derringer.

172

"Only if you put yours away, too," Mitchum said. "I don't want to hurt a woman, but I will if you try to shoot me. I—I thought I'd killed you once."

"I don't want to hurt anyone," she said, and pointed her derringer away from his body. "Come on," she urged.

Mitchum dropped his aim and slid his pistol back into his holster. What should he do?

Suzanna smiled and tucked the derringer back in between her breasts, reaching through the coat and shirt. "You know, James, I'm not really one of them—I'm not like the others—not like Lloyd. I'm just his woman—for now. I hate him, though, and was going to try to escape. But I've never been able to. Until now. If you help me—"

"I wish I could talk," Mitchum said, "but I've got to run. Stay here and don't move until I come back."

She nodded as he ran toward the express car. Suzanna sighed and forced herself to look down at the floor. She'd been avoiding it since she had glanced quickly at the bodies before falling to the ground to save her life. To her right Robinson lay on his back, his face distorted by the painful death he must have suffered. Chuck Willis was to her left, and she saw the reddish black hole that pierced his forehead.

Suzanna caught the stench of blood and gagged. She hurried into the club car in a rush to put as much distance as she could between herself and the two dead men who'd shared her bed.

Mitchum looked up as the door of the private car opened and Lloyd stood in front of him. Before the detective could fire his weapon Lloyd sneered and blasted a round into the man's heart. Mitchum's body

173

jerked back as he emitted a short cry, then fell dead next to Robinson.

Lloyd turned his back and covered his ears. The dynamite released its fury a few seconds before he'd expected. Once the glass had settled he tore through the door, Colt in hand ready for the express man. He kicked in the bowed door and slammed a bullet into the man who stared out at him in shock and surprise. The express man stumbled backward and fell lifelessly to the floor. A nearly empty whiskey bottle sat beside him on the floor next to his rifle.

The safes, Lloyd thought. Where were they? He looked around and found them lined up side by side. Working quickly, Lloyd removed eight sticks of dynamite from his vest pocket, unwrapped them from their cloth coverings, then lodged two in each safe's handle. He straightened out the fuses, then reached for his matches.

Spur made his way to the train. Damn that Mitchum, he thought. Maybe Lloyd had shot him, or maybe the bastard was hiding in a corner somewhere until the shooting stopped.

He ran along the tracks, his boots slapping the newly laid wet ties in perfect rhythm. Spur made it to the train, passed the caboose and express cars, then jumped up on the stairs beside Helena's car. He saw the blasted door as he swung up before it, and then saw Lloyd crouched in the car, his back to Spur. He drew his ice cold weapon and fired just as Lloyd looked up and lunged to one side. The bullet struck Lloyd's thigh. The man roared in pain and blasted one round that caught Spur in his left shoulder.

A split second later the train's air brakes snapped on and the express car jolted forward. Spur, still dazed by the bullet in his body, fell forward, hitting his forehead against the express car's door. He looked up, stunned, lying on his belly as his shoulder burned and his vision pulsated in watery images before him. He couldn't focus properly as he held himself up on one hand, his gun still gripped in the other. Damn it! he thought. Have to see. Have to shoot. Now!

Lloyd lit a match and touched it to two of the fuses, which sparkled in a series of tiny explosions, then unlocked the door and raced out the back of the express car toward the caboose. The two explosions would set the other dynamite off, and they should blow the detective to pieces, Lloyd thought.

Spur smelled the stench of black powder. He heard the fizzling fuses but saw only a bright patch of moving light. Got to run! Spur thought. He stumbled from the car, ignoring the pain that stabbed through his body from the bullet in his shoulder.

He'd made it to the connector before the first stick exploded. The other seven went moments afterwards, shaking the car as Spur moved toward the private car. He felt a few fragments hit his back but his thick clothing protected him against injury. Wincing, holding his aching left arm close to his body to minimize the pain that his every movement caused, Spur laid himself flat against the express car's exterior, next to the door, and waited.

After ten seconds he peered into the car. Lloyd bent before the safes. As Spur turned and lifted his six-gun he felt something hard press against his spine.

"You move one hair," Suzanna said, "and I'll blow you to bits."

Suzanna Buckland, Spur thought. Wasn't she dead?

"Go ahead, Lloyd!" she called. "Get the gold!"

The man didn't hesitate. The dynamite had loosened the doors. Lloyd kicked the first door to one side. He took three leather bags from the mail area and stuffed sacks of the double eagles into them. Five bags fit snugly in each.

"Is that all?" Suzanna asked as Lloyd rose and picked up the heavy bags. Snow fell heavily outside, whistling into the express car on icy winds.

"No. We're leaving the rest. Come on!" He leaped off the train but his legs buckled under the gold's weight as he landed. The three sacks jerked his body back and forth as they swung. Lloyd dropped them and one of the smaller bags of coins burst and spilled gold onto the snow.

Assuming that Suzanna would look at the yellow rounds of money lying on the white snow Spur spun and knocked the derringer from her hand. It discharged into the air as it flew away.

Spur aimed for Lloyd but Suzanna shoved him as he fired, sending the bullet driving harmlessly into the snow. Spur grabbed Suzanna, wrestling with her, trying to get an aim on Lloyd while she twisted and squirmed.

"Grab it up!" she yelled to Lloyd from the car. She slapped Spur's face and dug her fingernails into his cheeks.

Lloyd looked down, picked up one large bag and

hurriedly rose, then disappeared before Spur could get a shot.

He released the woman, cursing her, and ran down the steps into the snow after Lloyd. His boots had made unmistakable tracks in the snow.

"No, goddamn you!" Suzanna cried from above. "Don't take my gold!"

Spur hurried past it after Lloyd, reloading his six-gun. The snow continued, falling heavier and thicker, and soon Spur could barely distinguish the man in front of him.

Once the detective was gone, Suzanna walked down the steps and scooped up the gold coins. There might be a thousand dollars worth of them, she thought, and they were hers!

Then she looked around her. She was in the middle of a severe snowstorm, in the mountains. Her horse wouldn't be able to take her far, if she made it to him. How could she hide the money? She couldn't stay on the train if she kept it.

Suzanna stuffed a few coins in her pockets, left the bags and rest of the money on the snow, and climbed back onto the train. She sniffed and the cold bit at her, urging her back to the warmth inside.

Then she remembered Phoebe.

The poor girl, Suzanna thought, shivering out in this snow storm, probably not budging, wondering what's taking them so long. She'd freeze to death!

Suzanna turned back to walk down the steps, determined to find Phoebe.

"What the hell—who are you?" a man's voice said from behind her.

Suzanna turned and saw a man finely dressed in a black suit, a pipe dangling from his mouth. He held a gun.

"I'm—I'm—" Suzanna didn't know what else to do, so she slumped to the floor in a feigned swoon before the astonished man.

CHAPTER EIGHTEEN

Snow flurried around him and the wind howled as Spur followed Lloyd's tracks through the snow, which lay three feet deep on the ground in the area. Lloyd was somewhere above him on the hill.

As he walked his shoulder pounded, blood flowing freely from the gunshot wound. Spur felt his left arm go numb and his shoulder burn deep inside as he pressed against the area through his clothing, still trudging through the area. Spur shook his head to keep the flakes from collecting on it. With a wind chill that must have been at least twenty below, Spur knew he couldn't last more than a half hour without better clothes.

Spur climbed over a fallen tree frosted with snow. A blanket of white seemed to have dropped around him, bright but opaque, the snow effectively blocking his vision in all directions. But the trail made by Lloyd's passage showed clear below him. As long as the snow didn't fall much heavier he'd be able to follow it. He noticed a bright red spot on the snow, then another.

Lloyd was wounded. Why didn't the man give himself up? Spur's ears turned a bright pink and the cold air made his lungs scream as he continued following Lloyd.

He peered into the white light swirling around him. Spur knew he couldn't be more than fifty feet behind Lloyd. He thought about calling out the man's name, then rejected the idea. McCoy didn't want to give away his position.

A particularly fierce blast of icy air buffeted Spur as he walked through the trees and climbed the snowy hill. Lloyd wasn't in the best shape, he thought, then grimaced as his shoulder ached again and he remembered his own condition. Maybe he'd track Lloyd until he was tired or the cold killed one or the both of them. Spur shook his head, feeling energy drain from his body as blood slowly leaked out. If only this goddamn snow would stop falling long enough for him to take a good look around!

The wind sculpted the snow into fantastic shapes with sweeping lines around trees and boulders. The aspens, shocked at the last winter, stood rigidly still, their leaves and branches frozen in a thin coating of rain that had quickly turned to ice.

Spur grabbed a pine trunk and pulled himself up the hill. Where the hell could Lloyd be heading? Nowhere—unless he was going to his new hideout, or maybe the horses that had to be hidden somewhere. That must be it.

He hoped that Mitchum had found the gold and returned it to the train my now. Spur'd be damn miserable if the Union Pacific lost even one dollar from the shipment.

Spur's hands, feet and face were numb from the sub-freezing temperature. He continued his trek up the hill, using whatever means he could to help his ascent. Spur reached for an aspen trunk two feet from him. His powerful fingers locked around the tree and he put his weight behind it as he pulled himself up the hill, his feet refusing to function properly. The aspen bent and then broke. Spur's boots slipped on the snow and his chin bounced as he landed face down on his left shoulder. Spur groaned in pain as he slid backward down the hill.

He tightened his legs and pushed his feet against a tree to halt his slide, then lay for a moment resting on the slope, eyes closed. Each breath made his lungs ache, then crystallized as he exhaled. Pain pounded through his body.

As he pressed against the snow, unable to rise, the blackness that his closed eyes produced was inviting after the endless blinding white.

Have to get up, he told himself. Have to move. Don't go to sleep.

Spur's energy ebbed with the blood that flowed from the wound then froze as it oozed through his clothes. He relaxed against the snow, not bothering to brush off the flakes that collected on his face and stuck to his skin and eyelashes. Pain, exhaustion and the endless cold gently persuaded Spur's mind to slip.

He dozed for a moment, recuperating, seduced by the cold. He woke with a start. Someone shook him. Lloyd? Spur thought, groggy. The pain returned. Had Lloyd come back to kill him?

Spur forced his eyes open and was blinded by snow. He brushed off his lashes.

"Mister? Mister!" a woman's voice said.

As his eyes focused and the snow melted into them Spur recognized Phoebe, the woman who'd undressed for him in the mine. She was bundled against the snow, only her face visible peering from a fur-lined jacket. A half frozen horse stood by.

"Thank God you woke up," Phoebe said.

"Where's Lloyd?"

She frowned. "Stand up. You're gonna die if you just lay there in the snow." She brushed him off.

As Spur stood every pain renewed itself in a wild orgy of torture. "Where's Lloyd?" he asked again, weak.

"I don't know. I thought you were him when I first saw you," she said. "I was waiting for them with the horses but they never came back. And it got so cold! I was sure they should have been back by now, so I got worried and came out here. On my way I spotted you. Is he still alive?"

"Lloyd?" Spur nodded. "Last time I saw him he was. Unless the snow's killed him by now."

"What—what about my sister?"

"She's alive—at least she was the last time I saw her."

"Are we in any trouble?" Phoebe asked as Spur moved around, whipping up his blood, increasing his circulation.

"I don't know," Spur answered honestly. "Go on back to the train," he said, panting. "See your sister and find Mitchum or any of the railroad employees. Tell them you saw me and that I'm after Lloyd. I'll be back."

Spur looked around him. How long had he lain in the snow? He knew the trail was straight up but couldn't see the tracks—even the marks on his rapid descent had nearly been covered over with fresh snow. He cursed.

"It's too cold out here," Phoebe said, shivering. "Forget Lloyd. He's probably already dead." Her voice betrayed no emotion save that of urgency. "Come show me where the train is," she said.

"No. You go. I'll be fine." Spur started his slow ascent.

"Be careful!" Phoebe turned and mounted the horse, then rode off toward the tracks.

Spur cursed his pain while climbing. Where had Lloyd gone? Was he dead, or had he found a horse? Had Phoebe left the horses there just in case someone returned? He hadn't asked her, and it was too late now.

Since the snow had covered Lloyd's tracks Spur wondered if he'd find him before the bitter cold and snowstorm drove him back onto the train.

McCoy wasn't a quitter, and hated the idea of giving up, but at least he'd have the satisfaction of knowing that Lloyd wouldn't live long outside.

"Come on, McCoy," he said to himself. "Straighten up." He ignored the pain and climbed the hill.

"Miss Fredrickson! Miss Fredrickson!" a man called as he ran through the club car, dodging drinking passengers grumbling to one another about the delay.

"Yes?" She stood and went to the man, her heart pounding.

"Come quick!"

She hurried after him, ending in her private car, of all places. She saw the two draped forms on the floor again and shuddered, then looked at the strangely dressed woman sitting in her best chair while a man held a gun pointing at her.

"What on earth is happening here?" she asked the man in her usual demanding tone.

"I was sitting around waiting for the train to get underway again, and had the idea I could help out. So I started looking around and found this woman outside your car. I figured—the way she was dressed and all—she was one of the robbers, so I've been watching her ever since."

"I see."

"And since the train detective's dead I asked the conductor and he told me the other detective, Spur McCoy, is missing, so I should contact you."

"What?" she said, gasping. "James Mitchum is dead?"

The man nodded. "If that's the detective's name, that's right. What do you want to do with her?"

"I'll decide that. Thank you. I'll handle this now."

"You're quite welcome." The man bowed sharply and walked off.

As she stood looking at the woman, she remembered what Spur had said about the Lloyd gang—two members were women, both red haired. Was this one of them? If so, what was she doing here?

"What's your name?" she asked.

"Mary MacDonald," came the obviously southern voice.

Helena laughed in spite of the solemnity of the

situation. "I'd say it's Buckland—Suzanna, or is it Phoebe?"

She looked at Helena in surprise. "Suzanna. How do you know that?"

"It's my business to know, Miss Buckland. I'm a Union Pacific detective."

The southern woman burst out laughing, then quickly covered her mouth. "Really? I thought you were joking."

"I'm quite serious."

"It's the last thing I expected you to say." Suzanna calmed down and shook her head. "Well hell, you know who I am, so you know I was a member of Ray Lloyd's gang. But I never killed anyone and I never stole anything." Her eyes opened wide and she pulled a handful of gold coins from her pockets. "Except this."

Helena looked at it and frowned. "Did you pick this up from the bag that spilled outside?"

"Yes."

"I see."

"But I only did it because I've lived with that damned Lloyd for all these months and he never gave me a red cent—he wouldn't even let me buy my own clothes." She gestured to her masculine outfit and chuckled, then handed the money to Helena, who accepted it.

As she spilled the gold out onto a small table Helena felt a little thrill. "All right. I'm sure we can be lenient with you, since you brought this back and didn't try to escape. Besides, I can't quite believe you ever helped Lloyd rob trains."

"I never did—this was the first time."

"I see."

"So what happens now?"

"What happens?" Helena echoed.

Suzanna held out her hands. "Do you lock me up or can I get a drink and talk with you?"

"I—I have no idea," Helena said. "I'm new at this."

Suzanna laughed. "So am I."

The snowfall hadn't abated in the three minutes that Spur struggled through it up the hill. The ground became increasingly higher and his steps more dogged and taxing as millions of snowflakes melted partially together or simply lay on top of each other. Spur wished them all in hell when he stopped, exhausted.

The wind died down, and the snow fell with a lilt, not the blast of the past few minutes. As he leaned against a tree, panting, colder than he'd ever been, his breath turning to clouds and his shoulder screaming with pain, the tips of his fingers and nose nearly frost-bitten—Spur heard a groan to his right.

He pushed off from the tree and stumbled as quietly as he could through the still soft snow toward the groan. The sound wasn't repeated, so Spur trudged more quickly toward it, hoping that Lloyd made it and not some half-iced mule-deer.

Then he heard it again. It was unmistakably human. Spur drew his Colt. He still couldn't see anything so he crashed on by a huge tree. To its right he saw a gigantic thrust of rock, and at the rock's base Ray Lloyd knelt, huddling against the cold, a large canvas bag next to him. He rubbed his hands together while his lips murmured. Spur aimed.

"The game's over," Spur said heavily. "Time to go home."

"Not you!" Lloyd said, glancing up at Spur in terror.

"Yeah." Spur motioned with the Colt through the drifting snowflakes.

"No way. I'm not gonna rot in some prison or drop on a rope," Lloyd said, still rubbing his hands together on his thighs. Spur shook.

Spur shook his head at the pitiful man. Lloyd's hands suddenly reached between his legs and came up with his pistol. As he brought it up, Spur's Peacemaker roared. The round hit the back of Lloyd's gun hand, splattered blood and tissue over the hogsleg and spun it away into the snow. "Let's go back to the train," Spur said.

"No fuckin' way! I'm not going back with you. You're dying and I'm heading to the cabin!" His voice was wild with desperation.

"I saw Phoebe," Spur said. "She let the horses run free after I told her you were dead. You can't walk back, Lloyd. Come on. Drop the gun and we'll go to the train where we'll warm up."

"Damnit, no!" Lloyd shouted. "Why'd you have to fuck it all up, damn you? This was going to be my last, best, most successful robbery. You've wrecked my whole life, Spur! This was going to be my last job!"

"Hey, I'm crying for you, Lloyd! Let's go get some whiskey into us on the train."

"No!"

"You're nearly dead," Spur said, brushing snow off his head and shoulders. "Come on. Hell, if you want to shoot it out, we'll do it there. I'm tired of this fuckin' snow, Lloyd, and damn cold.''

Lloyd shook his head and lay on the snow. "No way, asshole. If I'm going down I'm taking you with me, after what you did to me today nothing else matters but seeing you dead." He drew a knife from his belt and threw it at Spur.

As it sped toward him Spur darted left and blasted a round into Lloyd's chest. The man's eyes closed, his face unsurprised, almost peaceful as his heart exploded and his consciousness dimmed. The outlaw opened his eyes for a moment, frowned, then dropped lifelessly to the snow. As he landed a gold double eagle rolled from his pocket onto the snow.

Spur bent to retrieve it, frowned at the coin, then lifted the bag of gold and headed down the mountain. He'd carry Lloyd's body with him but knew if he did he'd never make it to the train.

CHAPTER NINETEEN

Phoebe Buckland jumped from her mount beside the train, patted its mane sadly, then hurried toward the steps. Once inside she felt the warmth flush through her body, then cried out.

"Suzanna!" she said.

"Phoebe!" They hugged. "What on earth are you doing here? I thought you'd be back at the cabin or—or—" Suzanna shook her head. "Here, let's move by the heater." They walked through the club car.

"I couldn't stop worrying about you," she said, her eyes moist, "so I rode out here. I found the detective we caught—he was nearly dead in the snow. I think he went to find Ray. And—" Phoebe was out of breath.

"Slow down," Suzanna said. "Catch your breath and warm up, then talk."

"How—how are Steve and Chuck?" Phoebe asked as she rubbed her hands together.

"They're—they're dead, Phoebe. They died in the robbery."

Phoebe pushed back her shoulders gently. "I thought so. I'm just glad you're not."

"I nearly was. Twice, Phoebe. Can you feature that? I nearly got killed today not once, but twice!"

"You almost sound as if you enjoyed it!" Phoebe said half seriously, studying her sister's face.

"No, of course not," she said, shivering at the thought. "But it's out of my system—I don't need any more adventures and excitement. I'm ready to settle down and relax now that I've had my wild days."

"Did you get any gold for us?" Phoebe asked hesitantly.

Suzanna blushed and shook her head. "No. That was part of my plan to make sure we don't get thrown in jail."

"Then we're broke?" Phoebe asked. "That means we'll have to ride back to the cabin to get the money you've kept."

She shook her head. "No need to. I have it right here." She patted her bosom.

Phoebe's eyes widened with delight. "Suzanna, how did you know to bring it today?"

"I had a feeling, I guess." She shook her head. "I don't know. But I did it and that's what's important."

"How much do you have?"

"Four hundred and fifty dollars."

Phoebe gasped. "Four hundred fifty dollars? And I thought we were broke!"

"Yes. And if I let father know what's happened to us—how we were *kidnapped* and forced into a robbery attempt, I'm sure he'll wire us more. Especially if I tell him we need it to go back home to him."

"Suzanna!" she said, rubbing her cheeks. "How wicked! You don't mean to go back, do you?"

"No. But he'll give it to us anyway, and I'm not sure he wouldn't know that we planned not to return. When we get the new money we'll be able to stay longer in San Francisco."

Phoebe smiled. "That seems like a dream right now—sunny San Francisco, where it never snows. I'm freezing and you're dressed like a man."

"There's an awful lot of lonely men in San Francisco," Suzanna said with meaning.

"In three or four days I think some of them won't be so lonely anymore." Her face darkened. "Are you sure we won't get into any trouble?"

She smiled. "What did we do? Besides, we're women and we're practically sacred out here. Except to men like Lloyd." Suzanna laughed musically and threw an arm around her sister's neck. "Oh, Phoebe! Think of the fun we'll have. We'll spend all our money, get a ticket back home, and then set Dallas on its ear with gossip. Or maybe we'll just settle down, find some rich men to take care of us. Either way, Phoebe, I have a feeling the excitement's just starting —but a good kind of excitement. We'll have such a good time, Phoebe! Think of it!"

Phoebe smiled, and she welcomed the warmth as it moved through her body like a million stinging nettles.

Spur took three steps and collapsed face down on the two-foot deep snow. He looked wearily up and noticed that the snow had stopped falling. In the distance fifty feet, almost hidden by the trees, he saw the train.

Have to get up, he told himself. Have to move to the train. He pushed onto his hands and knees, then painfully swung a leg below him and started to rise. It buckled beneath him and Spur fell in a tangled heap.

"If we don't move now, Miss Fredrickson, we'll probably be stuck here for a day at least. The storm's heading west—where we're going. We can get through now—but I don't know if we can an hour from now. The snow's falling heavier up ahead, looks like."

"We can't just leave Mr. McCoy out in the snow to freeze to death!" Helena said. "I don't care if you are the engineer—I won't let you kill that man!"

"It's too cold to send out a search party," the engineer said. "If we don't get this baby moving we all may freeze to death. What do you think he'd want you to do?"

She flared at the comment, then reflected while the engineer lit his pipe. "I don't know. I haven't gotten to know him well."

"Then as engineer of this train, I say we move out now."

Helena paled. She turned to look out the window. Though the snow had stopped falling it was all she could see in any direction—a mass of white.

"I'll go out looking for him then!" she said stubbornly.

"He's probably already dead," the engineer said quietly. "Besides, I won't let you. This isn't just to protect you, Miss Fredrickson. Your father would fire me if I let you hurt yourself!"

Helena screwed up her face. "I'm going to cry," she said. "Are you happy?"

"Outstandingly so." He turned to walk back to the engine.

*　*　*

Spur nearly vomited with pain as he rose to his feet again. His left shoulder and arm were virtually useless, numb and aching. His balance straightened out and he lifted the gold bag, then stepped forward. Just fifty feet, he told himself. Twenty steps.

He occupied his mind with memories of endless deserts, days of such intense heat he bathed in his own sweat. Warmth and renewed energy flushed his body. Spur's legs worked automatically as he turned all his attention toward reaching the train. Snow began to fall again.

He passed the last few trees as the engine hissed and the whistle penetrated his brain, sounding unreal in his semiconscious condition. Spur ran, drugged with pain, his feet sinking into the blue snow around his boots, the forty pound sack of gold weighing him down.

The train inched forward as the whistle screamed again. Spur pushed himself to the limit, knowing he'd pass out from the exertion but not caring, knowing that all that mattered was reaching the train.

He ran up to it, paced alongside, his brain pounding, then found the energy to lift his two hundred pounds to the steps between the express car and Helena's coach. He gripped the cold iron, then dropped to his knees on the top step as the train steamed up the mountains.

Spur half pulled himself across the little vestibule and rested, leaning against the express car's shattered door, panting while his breath hung in clouds before him.

The other door opened. "Spur!"

He saw Helena walk toward him, then scream, terrified by the frost crystals that festooned his moustache, eyebrows and sideburns, and his bluish skin color.

Spur staggered forward past an incredulous Helena into the train. All he wanted was a shot of whiskey—warm whiskey.

An hour later Spur lay shivering in Helena Fredrickson's car while a doctor gently extracted the bullet from his shoulder. The sawbones applied an ointment and wrapped the wound tightly.

"Don't lift any heavy weights for a few days and you'll be fine," the doctor said. "Get some rest."

"Sure am glad you were on board," Spur said, slurring his words from the whiskey they'd poured down him.

"Always happy to be of service to the Union Pacific," he said. The doctor helped Spur back into his shirt and put his tools into his leather bag. He left, tipping his hat to Helena, who had stood at the rear of the car, not watching.

When he was gone she went to Spur.

"Does it hurt?" she asked.

"Only when I breathe," Spur laughed at the joke. "No, it's not too bad. I'll be fine."

She stood next to him looking down with concern. "Spur McCoy, I take back everything I ever said about you."

"Forget it, Helena," he wheezed.

"No, I mean it!" Her eyes were alive with admiration. "I thought you didn't know what you were doing. I should have known father would deal with a professional. If you hadn't been here, the gold would have been stolen and—"

"Forget it," he said.

"I guess I was jealous of you, because I wanted your job. That's why I didn't like you at first."

"And you took it out on me."

"You think you have me figured?" she asked.

"Yes."

Helena slapped his arm gently. "That should be interesting. I'd like to hear about me sometime."

"What about now?"

"No. The doctor said you should rest, and I think you could use a good sleep. I'll be here. We can move you off the train when we—"

"No. Nothing doing! I'm watching the gold until we reach Sacramento."

"Sorry," she said. "That's my job now. Without you or James Mitchum—" Helena paused. "Well, you know what I mean."

"Yeah, but I'm not going to let you do it alone." Spur's brow furrowed. "Where's the gold? You told me it was all recovered, but you never said where it was. The safes were blown. Where did you put it?"

"It's safe. It's hidden where no one will ever find it. I moved it an hour before you came back to the train."

"Where?"

"Don't worry. Just sleep now. We'll talk about it later."

"Tell me!" Spur thundered, then grimaced in pain.

"Okay. It's right under you." She kicked the bed leg.

"You put it under the bed?"

"Not quite."

"Damn you, Helena, stop giving me riddles! Where's the gold?"

She pouted. "It's *in* the bed. Below you."

Spur shook his head. "I don't know—"

"I'll show you later."

"But in your bed?" he asked, stunned.

"Of course. I don't let just anyone in there." She bent and kissed Spur's lips gently. "Sleep, love. We'll talk about it later."

Spur didn't complain. He pressed down against the gold and felt his body melt into the soft mattress. In moments, Spur enjoyed a dreamless sleep.

"Miss Fredrickson?" Suzanna said as the woman approached her.

"Yes?"

"Could you reassure my sister that we won't be charged with any crimes?"

She sighed. "Yes, but you may have to answer some questions. By the way, do you have enough money to cover your fares to—wherever it is you're going?"

"San Francisco or Sacremento," Phoebe said.

"And we have the money," Suzanna interjected.

"Fine. Then there's no problem."

"I do have one other question," Suzanna said.

Helena sighed. "What is it?"

She pointed to her clothing. "Do you have any old dresses you could sell or loan me?"

She smiled. "Of course."

"Did you find out what happened to Lloyd?" Phoebe asked.

"He's dead, somewhere out in the snow."

"And the detective—Spur McCoy?"

"He's fine and resting. Excuse me, but I have some work to do. Enjoy the ride—and I'll get you some things to wear as soon as I'm finished filling out reports.''

''Thanks!'' Suzanna said cheerily.

The 182 rattled and clanged through the snow-drenched mountains, its cow catcher pushing the snow away. After four more torturous miles upward it rounded a peak and roared down the other side on a track that had been pushed clean by a snowplow.

Helena Fredrickson wrote the name of the train company, her name and company position, the date and train number in a careful hand, then sat back and thought. James Mitchum, dead. Steve Robinson, dead. Chuck Willis, dead. Ray Lloyd, dead. Vincent Glass, dead. Spur McCoy, injured, bullet in left shoulder. She recorded the incidents as thoroughly as she could, in a special supplement to the accident report the train company always maintained.

As she wrote Helena couldn't force from her mind the intoxicating taste of Spur McCoy's lips.

CHAPTER TWENTY

Spur's consciousness washed in a rhythm of movement and sound, a gentle shifting from side to side lulling him back into the blackness of sleep. But as his body was suddenly jarred he jolted awake and lay staring up at the rubbed wood ceiling, blinking. What time of day was it? Spur saw no sun shining on the ceiling. Night?

"How do you feel?" a soothing voice asked him. Seconds later Helena Fredrickson's smiling face moved into view.

"Fine," Spur said, ignoring the quiet throb in his shoulder. He hoped it was healing properly. "Where are we?"

"In my private car," she said, smiling.

"No. I mean, where's the train?"

"Somewhere on the way to Sacramento. Remember?"

He nodded, his head still fuzzy. Spur scratched the prickly stubble on his chin and frowned. "How long did I sleep?"

"About ten hours."

Spur groaned. "How's the gold? Any more robbery attempts?"

"No. And there won't be. Word will get around about what you did to the Lloyd gang and that should cut robbery attempts." She smiled. "Feel strong enough to sit up?"

"Sure," he said, and pushed his elbows back to support himself. As he did so his face screwed up with pain. He shakily sat and smiled. "Easy as pie."

Helena smirked. "Maybe you should lie still for a while longer."

"No, I'm fine. What about the women—Suzanna and Phoebe Buckland? Where are they?"

Helena's face flared with jealousy. "You want to know about them?"

"Of course," Spur said. "They were members of Lloyd's gang—at least inactive members. What did you do with them?"

"I haven't done anything. They have free run of the train, which is only right since they paid for their tickets."

"You certainly haven't told them where the gold is, have you?"

"No, of course not. I'm not telling them anything about the gold, them or anyone else!"

"Good." He frowned. "Sorry, I'm still asleep. Besides, they're both women—they could never steal the gold."

Helena nearly exploded, but kept calm. "Damn you, Spur," she said softly. "I'm a woman. Belle Starr is a woman! Why can't you see that there's more to women that just—"

"All I meant was that they're two women, apparently unarmed, riding a train. It's hard to imagine they'd rob it after all that's happened." Spur's face grew dark. "How long was I out cold?"

"About ten hours."

"And did you stand beside me all those ten hours?" Spur asked with a playful smile.

"No. I had work to do. Why, are you disappointed?"

"No. Did you lock the door?"

"Yes. I wouldn't leave two treasures like you and the gold lying around where just anyone could walk in and take them from me."

Spur smiled at the compliment, then shook his head and struggled to move off the bed.

"What if those two nice ladies—the Buckland sisters—slipped in here when you were off god-knows-where writing your reports, stole every last double eagle, then left the train at the next stop? If they did it right, we wouldn't know till we were in Sacramento."

"But they couldn't get the gold without moving you," Helena argued. "It's not likely."

"I was so shot up, frozen and dead tired they could have dumped me on the floor and I wouldn't have felt it." Spur succeeded in moving his legs over the edge of the bed and, bent at the waist, slid forward slowly. He stood and turned around, then tried to lift the mattress.

"Let me help you with that," Helena said. "You're not supposed to lift anything."

Together they raised the mattress and pushed it half off the platform.

"Nothing," Spur said.

Helena reached into the bedbox and pushed down one side of the flat piece of wood. The other end popped up, revealing a hollow box two feet deep by six feet long. Spur whistled as he looked at the rows of double eagle stuffed bags. A fortune—he'd been sleeping on a fortune.

"Daddy had it specially built in case we needed to secrete something, but he didn't put the gold there this trip because he didn't want to endanger me."

"You were right," Spur said. "It's still there."

They remade the bed and Spur sat painfully on it, then lay back down. He felt the blood rush anew to his wound.

But he also smelled Helena's heady perfume. The soft, natural scent of woman, Spur thought, and inhaled again.

"Of course I'm right," she said. "I'm always right. I'm a woman."

Spur laughed. "Okay, Miss Fredrickson. I call a truce. You know, I was wondering."

"Wondering? About what?" Her face was open and radiant.

"How many men have you had in this bed?"

"Mr. McCoy!" Helena shrieked in pretended shock. "Really! I could never tell you that."

"Why not?"

She lifted her eyebrows. "Because I haven't kept count."

"Does your father know what you do on these train trips?"

Helena giggled. "No. He never hears a word."

"Then come here."

She shivered. "Why?"

"You'll find out."

She moved and sat beside him on the bed.

"Give me your hand," he said. She put hers—soft, tender—into his chapped paw. He grasped it from the top and moved it, then pushed it down hard on his spongy groin. "Feel that?"

Helena's voice shook. "Yes. Oh, yes!"

It stirred, expanding in length and width.

"Feel what you're doing to me?"

"Uh-huh!"

Spur looked at Helena's face. Her eyes were shut, lips parted, her full concentration turned toward what she felt. Grinning, he moved one hand and touched her knee, then hiked up her dress until his fingers drove under it. He reached in and to his astonishment felt her bare leg. Helena Fredrickson wore nothing under the simple black dress.

"I've been waiting for you to touch me there," she said.

He smiled again as he found her crotch. Helena's body shook as he pushed his fingers up into her, making her gasp, then rubbed her clitoris with his thumb.

Her hand tightened over his penis, outlining it against his pants, gently squeezing the head and feeling down to find his testicles.

Spur removed his hand from his crotch to work her over. Helena's hands were suddenly at his waist, unbuckling his belt and pulling it back, then unbuttoning his pants and pushing them down with his drawers. Spur's massive penis sprang up, making Helena cry out.

"God, what a man you are!" she squealed. Helena grasped the warm silky organ. "It feels so good."

"Tastes mighty good, too," he said, continuing to rub her button.

She smiled and licked the head. Flames flashed across his shaft as she tongued him. He gently pushed his hips upward, slipping his penis between Helena's lips and into her warm mouth.

She gagged slightly as it hit the back of her throat, but swallowed and Spur groaned as he slipped momentarily down her constricting throat. With one hand she caressed his balls, pulling at their hairy sack and twirling his dark crotch hairs between her fingers.

Helena groaned and climbed on the bed, turned, then squatted above Spur's head. Without releasing him from her mouth she lowered herself until his mouth contacted her groin.

Spur licked at her mystery, sucking at her juices and chewing on her clitoris. Helena moaned deep in her throat as she sucked his penis while he spread her lips wider and thrust three fingers up her as his tongue slashed against her button.

Helena's bottom writhed as they ate each other. She pulled her head from his crotch and licked her lips.

"I want you inside me," she said hungrily, with a sexual passion that surprised Spur.

He tried to move but his shoulder ached. She pushed down gently on him and turned around again. Lifting her dress she knelt over his crotch. He grabbed his stiff penis and held it at the appropriate angle.

Helena, her shoulders hunched forward, moved back and sat on him. Their flesh melted together in incredible sexual heat. Spur reached up and cupped her breasts under her dress as she bounced on top of him, her tight hole gripping and rubbing against him.

"Fuck me, Spur! Fuck me!"

"I'll fuck you," he said. He pushed her off him on her next upward stroke.

"What are you doing?" She asked, angry at the interruption as she slid off.

Spur stood, ignoring the pain in his shoulder, his throbbing penis jutting out before him. "Get that dress off, woman!" he barked. Damn the pain! He needed a good, hard roll to wake him up.

Helena's eyes glazed and she smiled before stepping out of the dress. Her body was as beautiful as her face.

"On your back," he said.

She obediently moved into position. Spur shrugged out of his clothes and, with his boots on, laid softly on top of her. He felt down and guided himself to her vagina, then pushed savagely, joyously into her. Helena's body shivered beneath his as he arched his back and withdrew, then plowed into her again.

Each time he hit home Helena moaned. Spur bent over to suck her breasts and she tossed her head from side to side, pressing momentarily against the mattress. Her hips rose to meet his, crashing together as their organs worked to blast them both to oblivion for a few fleeting seconds.

Spur's body slapped hers. The pain in his shoulder was forgotten. He rammed her wildly, then lifted her head and looked into her eyes.

"Helena?" he asked.

"Hmmm?" She opened her eyes for a second, then shut them.

"Look at me." Spur pulled out from her, his body poised above hers, the head of his penis a half-inch from her sheath.

She glared up at him, irritated. "What is it?"

"Nothing. I just wanted to look into your eyes while I slid back in." Spur's hips slowly contracted, pushing his penis forward. He watched every nuance of feeling pass in Helena's eyes as he rammed his oversized organ into her.

"Jesus. You're big!" she gasped.

"Thanks." He pumped, riding higher to rub against her clitoris as he entered and withdrew. Helena went crazy, mumbling, shivering, one hand pinching her nipple and the other travelling down to grip his butt. She spread her legs further apart, letting Spur sink in deeper still. Helena shook and rolled her way through a mind breaking orgasm.

Spur felt his own control about to burst and thrust harder into her. She sighed as he pounded and looked down at her, his eyes on her face, while he ejaculated.

Spur ground his hips against hers while he rocked through his pleasure. Exhausted by his sexual performance, Spur lay on her body, his left shoulder off her so that it didn't pain him.

"Oh, you'll hurt yourself," Helena said, panting. "Let me get up and you can lay back down again."

"I've got a better idea," Spur said. "Why don't we lay on our sides?"

She smiled. "Okay."

"But lay facing away from me," Spur cautioned.

Helena's grin grew. They moved into position and

Spur pushed his still rock-hard penis against her softly warm buttocks.

"Better?" she asked.

"Yes."

"Spur, did you want me the first time you saw me?"

He paused. "I want you right now." He moved his penis to lie within her valley.

"I'm serious."

He wrapped his arms around her and gripped her breasts. "So am I."

"Spur McCoy, damn you!"

He laughed. "Yes. Of course! How could you think anything else! You're a very attractive woman."

"Thank you." She snuggled back to him, then lifted a leg.

His penis shifted to her sex zone, and Spur couldn't resist angling his body into a better position. He slid his legs between hers and then drove up into her tight vagina.

"God!" she said. "I didn't know you could do it like this!"

"Too bad the trip to Sacramento's not longer," Spur said. "I could show you lots more."

She laughed and pushed back as he slid inside her again. Spur gripped her shoulders tenderly and rode her while the 182 rattled along the rails, belching coal smoke, as a whistle stretched out across the night.